W9-BPD-683

SOME PENGUIN PROBLEMS

ALSO BY DR. KATE BIBERDORF

Kate the Chemist: The Big Book of Experiments

*Kate the Chemist: The Awesome Book of
Edible Experiments for Kids*

Kate the Chemist: Dragons vs. Unicorns

Kate the Chemist: The Great Escape

Kate the Chemist: The STEM Night Disaster

Kate the Chemist: The Birthday Blastoff

SOME PENGUIN PROBLEMS

DR. KATE BIBERDORF

WITH HILLARY HOMZIE

Philomel Books

Hi! My Name is Dr. Kate Biberdorf,

but most people call me Kate the Chemist. I perform explosive science experiments on national TV when I'm not in Austin, Texas, teaching chemistry classes. Besides being the best science in the entire world, chemistry is the study of energy and matter, and their interactions with each other. Like how we can use salt and sand to prevent ice from forming on roads during a snowstorm! If you read *Some Penguin Problems* carefully, you will see how Little Kate the Chemist uses chemistry to solve problems in her everyday life.

But remember, none of the experiments in this book should be done without the supervision of a trained professional! If you are looking for some fun, safe, at-home experiments, check out my companion books, *Kate the Chemist: The Big Book of Experiments* and *Kate the Chemist: The Awesome Book of Edible Experiments for Kids*. (I've included one experiment from that book in the back of this one—how to make chocolate-covered pretzels!)

And one more thing: Science is all about making predictions (or forming hypotheses), which you can do right now! Will Little Kate the Chemist be able to use her science skills to solve the penguin problem? Let's find out—it's time for Kate the Chemist's fifth adventure.

XOXO,
Kate

PHILOMEL BOOKS
An imprint of Penguin Random House LLC, New York

First published in the United States of America by Philomel Books,
an imprint of Penguin Random House LLC, 2021

Copyright © 2021 by Kate the Chemist, LLC

Penguin supports copyright. Copyright fuels creativity, encourages diverse
voices, promotes free speech, and creates a vibrant culture. Thank you for
buying an authorized edition of this book and for complying with copyright
laws by not reproducing, scanning, or distributing any part of it in any form
without permission. You are supporting writers and allowing Penguin to
continue to publish books for every reader.

Philomel Books is a registered trademark of Penguin Random House LLC.

Visit us online at penguinrandomhouse.com.

Library of Congress Cataloging-in-Publication Data is available.

Printed in the USA

ISBN 9780593351277

1 3 5 7 9 10 8 6 4 2

LSCC

Edited by Jill Santopolo

Design by Lori Thorn

Text set in ITC Stone Serif

This book is a work of fiction. Any references to historical events, real people,
or real places are used fictitiously. Other names, characters, places, and
events are products of the author's imagination, and any resemblance to
actual events or places or persons, living or dead, is entirely coincidental.

The publisher does not have any control over and does not assume any
responsibility for author or third-party websites or their content.

For five fierce women in my life:
Kim, Kelsea, Caity, Jessica, and Gabi

TABLE OF CONTENTS

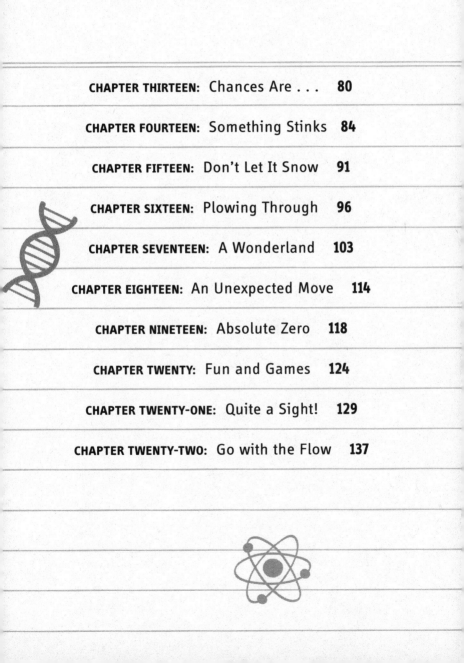

CHAPTER ONE

A SECReT TRiP

Convection (noun). A process that involves the transfer of heat. Basically, molecules in gases or liquids will really start moving and grooving. A burst of steam from your freshly made hot cocoa means that heat is transferring into the air.

I CAN KEEP A SECRET. At least that's what I told myself.

But it was next to impossible. After all, my best friend can practically read my mind. Her name is Birdie Bhatt, and we stood together in our school hallway the day after I found out. The morning bell was about to ring.

"C'mon, tell me, Kate." Birdie flicked her long hair over her shoulder. "You know something."

"Um, well . . . maybe." I glanced

at a nearby bulletin board. In rainbow letters it said *Throw Kindness like Confetti*. Telling your BFF a secret isn't just like telling anyone a secret. Especially when she's told you so many secrets herself. And she's a great secret-keeper too. A bunch of kids slogged past us in winter coats and backpacks. I yanked off my turquoise mittens. It was toasty warm inside the school.

Lowering my voice, I leaned forward and whispered the secret.

"I can't hear you." Birdie pulled off her mittens too. They were purple with swirls of silver. Which was typical of her unflashy-yet-artistic flair.

She pointed at the noisy first graders at the end of the corridor.

Stepping closer, I cupped my hand over my mouth. "Fifth grade is going on a field trip," I said in a low voice. "I overheard my mom talking about it yesterday afternoon." My mom just happens to be the principal of our school, so if I'm lucky, and quiet, I can overhear lots of secrets.

"Where are we going?" Birdie sounded as excited as I felt.

"Not sure. All I know is that it involves a looooong

bus ride." I couldn't help bouncing up and down right in the middle of the hallway. A long bus ride meant somewhere awesome and far away, like Detroit or Chicago.

"That's so cool about the field trip, but"—she paused—"I get car sick. And bus sick." She smiled, but it was wobbly. Suddenly I remembered what happened when my family took her up to the Tunnel of Trees in northern Michigan. The road twisted like a pretzel, and Birdie lost her lunch at a spot known as Horseshoe Curve.

"You won't get sick if you sit up front," I reminded her.

"You're right. And I can take those ginger chews. Do you know when we're going?"

"Nope, but I sure hope we go soon." I gestured at the window next to the double doors leading outside. A few flurries fluttered down. "We need to have something fun to look forward to. The month of January is way too long."

"Yeah. Unless we get some snow days."

"Don't even think about snowstorms right now," I said in a warning voice. We turned into the fifth-grade corridor. "For our field trip, we want perfect weather. Clear blue skies and white puffy cumulus clouds."

Cumulus clouds are the kind everyone draws. Especially Birdie. They look like fluffy cotton balls and form due to convection, which means a transfer of heat. You see, I'm all about chemistry. That's because you don't  just study it, you experience it. Chemistry is how snowflakes form crystals. Or how your muscles kick a soccer ball. It even explains why you feel bubbles of happiness when you know you're going on a field trip.

Our school, Rosalind Franklin Elementary, is named after one of the most famous chemists that ever lived. Learning about Dr. Franklin is how I got interested in science in the first place. She helped discover DNA, which is like the secret code for life. It carries all the info about how something will look and act, from dandelions to elephants to humans. It even decides whether someone will be prone to car sickness, like Birdie. Pretty much everything except not-alive stuff like water fountains has DNA.

"Please don't tell anyone." I took a sip of water from the fountain. "You know, about the field trip."

"I won't." Birdie held up her hand. "I swear on the

BFF code of honor." I sighed with relief because I knew the secret was safe with Birdie. She *never* breaks the BFF code of honor.

A few minutes later, we settled into our class. At first, I tried my very best to forget about the secret. Only it got hard. I kept on thinking more about our long trip. It had to be a city, and someplace indoors because of the winter weather. Both Chicago and Detroit had silver skyscrapers, and both of them were on the water. Detroit was on the Detroit River with views of Lake St. Clair. And Chicago was on one of the Great Lakes—Lake Michigan, one of the largest lakes in the world.

In my mind, I kept on picturing the jagged skyline and all of that shimmering water. Oh, it was so exciting! Usually, my family goes to Chicago or Detroit just a couple of times a year. In my seat, I tried to stay calm. But that became way too challenging when Mrs. Eberlin said she had a "special announcement" to make right after attendance.

Leaning back against her desk, she wore an extra-huge smile.

"Class, let's stop the chitchat," she said. "I have an amazing field trip to tell you about."

Birdie whipped around in her chair, and we exchanged looks. Oh wow! It seemed like our class trip was happening sooner rather than later. And that was just fine with me.

I definitely couldn't wait to find out where we were going.

CHAPTER TWO

What Contains the Answer?

Erlenmeyer Flask (noun). This is a special container that scientists use for a number of different things in a lab. It was designed by German chemist Emil Erlenmeyer, and its glass is so strong that he could do big chemical reactions inside the flask without worrying about it shattering. It has a ginormous name for a ginormous invention!

OUR TEACHER, MRS. EBERLIN, stood in front of the whiteboard. She pushed her glasses up on her nose and suddenly looked very serious. "In order to figure out where we are going on a very special field trip, you're going to have to do some work."

Some kids moaned. Others, like me, leaned forward expectantly.

7

"Told you, it's going to be special," I said softly to Birdie, whose desk was in the row in front of mine.

"Told you what?" asked Elijah Williams, who sat behind me. He's my next-door neighbor and my other closest friend. Immediately, I felt guilty about not telling him the secret.

"The field trip is going to be someplace cool and far away because we're going on a long bus ride," I whispered.

"Did you say *a long bus ride*?" asked Elijah in way too loud a voice.

"Shhhh!" said Birdie and I in unison. But it was too late.

"Kate knows we're going on a long bus ride!" shouted Memito Alvarez. "Tell us where we're going!"

Suddenly, everyone in the classroom was staring at me. My cheeks warmed.

"Kate, if you know where we're going, I'd appreciate you keeping it to yourself," Mrs. Eberlin stated. She put her hands on her hips in that teacher way that meant business.

"I actually don't know where we're going," I admitted.

"Yeah right, Kate." Shoving his floppy bangs out of his eyes, Jeremy Rowe glared at me. "She knows. And she's not telling."

"Actually, Kate really doesn't know where we are going," stated Birdie quietly, and I gave her a grateful look. Birdie might be shy, but she always stands up for what she believes in.

"Thanks, Birdie," I said. "Just because my mom's the principal doesn't mean I know everything."

Jeremy shook his head. Just last week, Jeremy had been sent down to the office for grabbing Mia Wong's cookie out of her lunch bag and taking a bite out of it. My mom had given him a talking-to, and for the past few days he had been giving me these withering looks.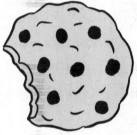

Sometimes having your mom as a principal is awesome. And sometimes it isn't.

"I bet we're going to Lansing," said Julia Yoon, who is our student body president and is good at knowing stuff like that. Lansing is the capital of Michigan, the state where we live. In fourth grade, Julia was the first kid to memorize all the states and their capitals.

"I think we're going to Detroit," I said. "There's tons of museums there."

"Nah, not a museum," said Elijah. "I bet it's the Binder Park Zoo. That one near Battle Creek."

"What about Greenfield Village?" said Avery Cooper. "You can visit an inventor's lab. Plus, they have people dressed up in costumes, so you get to learn history." Avery is a fan of anything to do with costumes and drama. Her dads run the theater in our town.

"Brrrr!" Phoenix Altman, Avery's best friend, rubbed her hands together. "It'll be too cold for the zoo or the village. I want to go someplace where we can be inside and toasty warm, like a museum."

On her desk, Birdie tapped her box of pastels. "I hope it's the Art Institute in Chicago. They have masterpieces there by Vincent van Gogh and Claude Monet and other famous artists."

"Those are all great guesses," said Mrs. Eberlin. "But none of you are right. To find the answer, we're going to solve a mystery." Mrs. Eberlin used a giant black dry-erase marker to write the number 8.1 on the board.

"What's that number?" asked Elijah.

"My sister's age," said Julia.

Memito held up eight fingers. "It's the number of slices of pizza I'm going to eat for lunch."

"Nope." Jeremy shook his head. "It's how many minutes school should last."

Some kids laughed, and Mrs. Eberlin tapped her watch. "When you love what you're doing, time really does fly," she said with just a hint of her Brazilian accent. When she gets excited, it shows up a little. "Like right now, I promise you time will whiz by. Because we're going to solve a mystery together. Just watch."

She reached under her desk and pulled out four Erlenmeyer flasks. Chemists use that kind of flask all the time. It has a narrow neck and a wide, flat bottom. You can put a stopper on the top if you need to swirl and swoosh a solution.

Personally, I love to do the swirling and the swooshing. When my dad makes homemade salad dressing in a jar, he always lets me shake it up.

It's one of the best ways to mix stuff.

"Now I need some volunteers," said Mrs. Eberlin. "Who wants to come up and help the class solve the mystery? Using some science. Chemistry, to be exact."

My hand shot up. "Me!" I shouted. "Please! Please! Please!"

CHAPTER THREE

GROW THIS ANSWER

Litmus Paper (noun). This is a piece of paper that has been treated with a special dye that changes color when it interacts with an acid or a base. When you dip it into a liquid, the paper will turn red if it's an acid or blue if it's a base. If only getting answers for my math test were this easy!

MRS. EBERLIN SCANNED THE CLASSROOM. "For our volunteer, I'm going to pick Elijah. He's waiting very patiently with his hand up."

Did that mean I wasn't patient? Probably.

With a grin, Elijah strode up to the front of the classroom.

"All right, here's the clue," said Mrs. Eberlin. "It

will help you all figure out just where we are taking our field trip. Think of yourselves like explorers or scientists about to make a discovery."

Almost everyone in the class was quiet. We studied our teacher, who stood up in front of her desk wearing an extra-big smile. "Okay, Elijah," said Mrs. Eberlin. "Open this box, take what's inside, and show the class." Elijah scooped something out of a small cardboard box. Then he held up three capsules that looked a little bit like my dad's vitamin pills. Only they were red, green, and blue.

"The capsules in Elijah's hand need the number 8.1"—Mrs. Eberlin tapped the number on the whiteboard—"in order to survive and thrive."

"Huh?" Phoenix dramatically slapped her hand on her forehead. "I don't get it."

"Me either," I admitted.

"These capsules are weird," said Elijah as he and I exchanged looks. We had no idea what our teacher was up to.

Next Mrs. Eberlin pulled little strips of purplish paper out of a jar. She waved them at us, and they made a little swishing sound. Mrs. Eberlin asked us to guess what the strips of paper were for.

"Little flags," suggested Avery.

"Teeth whitening," called out someone else.

And then, all of a sudden, I got it. My hand shot up.

Only Mrs. Eberlin called on Birdie, and I had to press my lips together to stop from blurting out the answer.

"The little strips would be perfect for drawing mini cartoons," said Birdie.

"For who?" asked Jeremy. "Hamsters?" A bunch of kids giggled along with Birdie.

I waved my hand in the air again.

"It looks like Kate might have the answer," said Mrs. Eberlin.

"Yes! Those are litmus strips," I said, "which is a fancy name for pH paper. They tell us whether something is an acid or a base. An acid is like lemon juice, and a base would be like dishwashing detergent."

"Exactly right, Kate." Mrs. Eberlin gazed around the room. "Okay, so I'm choosing some new volunteers." She pointed to Avery, then to Skyler Rumsky, who loped up front with his long strides. Then to Memito and me.

I yelped. "Wow-weee!" Then I raced up to Mrs.

Eberlin's desk. "What are we going to be testing?" I asked. When scientists test things, they always need to do it in a very systematic way. That just means it can't be all hodgepodge. My grandma Dort in Texas uses that word. *Hodgepodge* means a big mess.

Mrs. Eberlin brought out four beverages. "Okay, here's what you'll be testing!" She pulled out a bottle of lemonade, a Coke, a Snapple raspberry tea, a bottled water, and four flasks. Then she prepared each flask with one of the drinks.

Avery dipped the pH paper into the flask with the lemonade.

It turned red.

"What do you think that means?" Mrs. Eberlin asked.

Pretty much everyone said it was an acid. Then I mentally noted that acid meant red.

Next Skyler tested the Coke. It also turned red.

Memito picked the tea. More red.

"Is everything an acid?" asked Memito.

"Let's test the water and find out." I dipped my paper, and it turned blue. "That means this bottled water is basic."

"Exactly!" said Mrs. Eberlin. "Great job, everyone." Then she shooed us back to our seats. "So let's take a look at our results. The first three drinks turned the litmus paper red, but the bottled water turned the paper blue. Now, we already know that red means acid and blue means base, but each of these colors can *also* be represented by a number on something called the pH scale. On the pH scale, 1 is very acidic and 14 is very basic. Anything over 7 is considered basic." On the board, she circled 8.1. "So that number means . . ."

"Something that is just sort of basic," said Elijah.

"Man, that kind of sounds like an insult," said Memito. He waved his fingers at Elijah. "You're basic and boring." He yawned.

"Ha-ha," said Elijah.

Next Mrs. Eberlin asked for one more volunteer to help with the final step. Everyone wanted to do it. But Julia got to go up. She said she hoped that she didn't mess anything up. Mrs. Eberlin and a bunch of kids assured Julia that she would do a great job.

When Julia got to the front of the room, Mrs. Eberlin instructed her to put the three capsules in the water so we could see what needed the 8.1 in order to survive.

That meant something that would do well in water that was slightly more basic than acidic.

"You ready?" asked Mrs. Eberlin.

"I hope so," said Julia uncertainly. "Should I count to ten first?"

"That's a good idea," said Mrs. Eberlin.

"I bet something is going to explode," said Jeremy. "You better step back. Remember that baking soda experiment?"

"Or it could—poof—disappear like a magic trick," said Phoenix in a dreamy voice.

"Or make a lovely rainbow," suggested Birdie.

Julia counted backward from ten and then carefully dropped the capsules in the flask of water. Everyone anxiously leaned forward.

"Nothing's happening," moaned Memito.

"You guys, be patient," I said. "It's science."

While we were waiting, Mrs. Eberlin said she was going to hand out a code that would also help us solve the mystery.

She passed out a sheet of paper.

DEHS OT
GNIOG

It said: *dehs ot gniog.*

"Maybe it's in another language," said Julia.

"Is it in Portuguese?" asked Phoenix. After all, our teacher grew up in Brazil.

"Nope," said Mrs. Eberlin. "Portuguese is a Latin-based language, so it looks a lot like Spanish, Italian, and French."

"Wait a minute," Phoenix said. "You just said *Latin.* Maybe it's in Pig Latin."

"No, with that you move the consonant from the beginning of the word to the end of the word and add *ay*," I said. Dad taught us all Pig Latin just a few months ago. "So *Pig Latin* in Pig Latin is ig-pay atin-lay."

"Hmm." Elijah flipped the sheet around. He shook his head. "Reading it upside down doesn't help."

"But you're onto something," said Mrs. Eberlin.

"Wait! Because it's backward!" cried Elijah. "*Dehs ot gniog* means . . . going to shed."

"What?" asked Memito. "We're going to a shed?"

"There are lots of kinds of storage sheds," I mused. "Maybe it's a factory."

"Or a garden. That would be great," gushed Phoenix.

"I wish it was a shed for something awesome like an

airplane or a spaceship," said Elijah. "Maybe we're going to the Air Zoo Aerospace & Science Museum in Kalamazoo?"

"Well, keep on thinking about it," said Mrs. Eberlin. "Time to look back at those capsules."

This time the entire class crowded around our teacher's desk. I inched my way to the front.

"Tell me what you see," said Mrs. Eberlin. "You can also touch the capsules."

All at once, kids pushed to get closer. "One at a time," cautioned Mrs. Eberlin.

The red, green, and blue capsules had floated to the top. Now they were bigger and puffy and sort of shapeless.

Mrs. Eberlin used some tweezers to pull the blue and green ones out of the flask. When it was my turn, I tentatively reached out to touch the blue one. "It's sticky."

"I think there might be some sort of film on it," added Julia, who poked the green one with her thumb. She made a face.

Next Jeremy prodded the red capsule with the tweezers. It moved around the flask and puffed out even more.

"Look! It's turned into a different shape," I said.

"Hey, those look like those magic grow-a-pet thingies!" shouted Elijah. "When I was little, I had dinosaur ones."

"That's excellent sleuthing, Elijah," said Mrs. Eberlin, and the competitive part of me was just a smidge jealous. But mostly I was happy for my friend.

She put the green and blue capsules back into the flask and gave it a gentle swirl. Another minute later, the capsules looked like little sponges, but in three brand-new shapes. They were still too small to use as actual sponges to clean anything though.

With the tweezers, Mrs. Eberlin dramatically flicked them out of the flask one by one.

"That's a sea turtle!" Phoenix yelled, pointing at the green sponge.

"And the red one is a crab," added Julia. "Or maybe a lobster."

"Yes! A turtle and a crab," Mrs. Eberlin confirmed with a big smile.

"What's the blue one?" I wondered out loud.

"A dolphin?" guessed

Birdie as our teacher used the tweezers to unravel the blue sponge.

"It's a hammerhead shark!" screamed Jeremy. It was dead silent for a second before our classroom erupted in chatter.

"Are we going to Lake Michigan?" guessed Skyler.

"No," said Birdie. "That makes no sense. There aren't sharks in Lake Michigan."

"Or sheds," I said. "Remember that backward clue."

"Lifeguards use sheds," defended Jeremy, and he gave Skyler a high five. Only he had to stand on his tiptoes since Skyler was so tall. "I bet we're going to the ocean."

"That would be too long of a bus trip," said Julia. "My parents would never let me go."

"We're definitely not going to the ocean," said Avery, rolling her eyes.

Suddenly, Birdie's eyes lit up. "I figured it out," she announced. "We're going to the aquarium."

"But why the shed?" asked Avery. "That seriously doesn't make sense."

And then all at once, I got it. "It does if we're going to the Shedd Aquarium in Chicago!" I cried.

"That's right," said Mrs. Eberlin. "It's called the Shedd because it's named after the founder, John G. Shedd. He was the president of the Marshall Field's department store in Chicago, and he gave the money to start the aquarium."

That aquarium is so awesome. It's got dolphins. And jellyfish. Sharks. And most of all, rockhopper penguins, my favorite animal ever. They hop everywhere, make nests out of pebbles, and have the cutest little yellow feathers on their heads. Everyone started talking all at once.

Birdie and I were jumping up and down as Mrs. Eberlin handed out permission slips. She announced that in order for us to go on the field trip, she needed to have four parent volunteers from our class. "The field trip is going to be on Friday, January 28. So, a little over two weeks from now."

Wow. The field trip was happening soon. Today was Thursday, January 13. Not far away at all.

If only I had a time machine so that we could go to the aquarium tomorrow.

Oh well.

Looked like I'd just have to wait the regular way, along with everyone else.

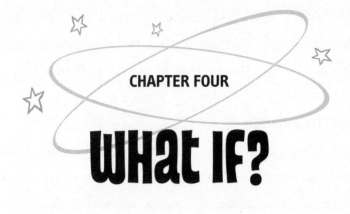

CHAPTER FOUR

WHAT IF?

Sedimentation (noun). This is the process of separating heavier matter from a solution in, say, a flask or beaker. But it works outside beakers too! Like how sand can be carried by a river and then deposited on its banks to make a perfect little beach. So every time you see a beach, you can thank sedimentation!

"THE AQUARIUM MIGHT BE the best field trip ever," I said to my friends during lunch at our usual table. It was the day after we had found out that we were going to Chicago. The cafeteria was noisy because it was Friday, when everyone got rowdy. Kids were chatting and laughing.

"When it comes to field trips, we've paid our dues," said Avery as she crunched into an apple.

24

"What is that supposed to mean?" asked Phoenix. Since she was her best friend, she didn't mean to directly challenge her—it was more like she was asking for clarification.

"We're in fifth grade," replied Avery, sounding wary and like her typical dramatic self. "So we've earned the right to go someplace *marvelous*."

"Yeah, not like that sewage treatment plant in fourth grade," said Memito, who took the last chomp of a celery stick dipped in hummus. "Remember that place?" He mock shivered. "If the aquarium is going to be stinky, at least it will have cool fish swimming around in it."

"Hey, I liked that water treatment place," I said. "And there were organisms there. They were just microscopic. Plus, all of those giant sedimentation tanks were so cool! Remember how gravity pulled particles to the bottom?"

"Ah, not really." Memito plugged his nose. "But I sure remember the stinky part."

"Well, I, for one, am certainly glad my dad is coming on the aquarium field trip," said Avery. "He adores taking photos. And there will be a lot more to see than sludge."

Avery's dad was the first parent to sign up as a

chaperone for the field trip. She had told us the good news this morning, and Mrs. Eberlin had looked super pleased. Her dad, who designs the posters for the local theater that he helps run, is like a semi-professional photographer. He always takes incredible shots whenever he goes on field trips.

"That's awesome your dad will take photos," said Birdie. "Maybe I can use them to make some paintings of the jellies!"

"Whoa, you're talking about the trip like it's a done deal," said Memito. "But it's not. Let's be real."

"Yeah," said Phoenix. "Mrs. Eberlin said we need at least four chaperones. So far, nobody else's parents have said they're going."

"Yet," said Elijah.

"But if nobody else steps up to the plate, we're doomed." Memito sighed heavily.

"My parents are busy," said Birdie.

Everyone else said pretty much the same thing. Except for Elijah. "I still need to ask," he admitted, sounding hopeful. "How about you, Kate?"

"Me?" I almost swallowed my carrot stick whole. "Yesterday, I had indoor soccer late, so I didn't get a chance to ask either." I was shocked that he even asked. And everyone knew exactly why.

CHAPTER FIVE

THE PARENT PROBLEM

Gas (noun). A gas has no fixed shape or volume. But when a gaseous state is under pressure, you sure will know. When you shake up a soda bottle and pop open the lid, tons of gas molecules fly into the atmosphere. Then they spread out quickly like first graders who have just been let outside for recess.

NOBODY WANTS MY MOM to go on a field trip.

She's the principal. Plus, our school is too small to have an assistant principal. So someone has to run the school. Since my little brother is a lot younger, my dad has always needed to be home to pick him up from preschool and watch him after that. So he couldn't go on field trips either.

But this year is different. Liam is in full-time kinder-garten so there's no reason my dad couldn't do it. I don't know why I hadn't thought about it.

"I'm sorry I didn't ask," I said, starting to feel guilty.

"Well, your dad is fine. But whatever you do, just don't ask your mom," said Jeremy.

"Otherwise, we won't be able to have fun," added Memito. "No paper airplanes on the bus."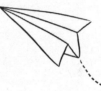

"Yeah, well, don't worry," I said in a defensive voice. I wouldn't ask her because she couldn't come anyway.

"I'll ask my dad," I said in my most upbeat voice. "I bet he can do it! He used to go on field trips with Liam's preschool class all the time. I'm *sure* we'll find enough chaperones. I mean, really, has a trip ever been canceled because of not getting enough chaperones anyway?"

"Yup," said Tala Campo, plopping down at the end of the table. "Sorry I'm late," she said. "But I had a den-tist appointment." Tala was new at school, but she was already one of my good friends. She moved to Michigan from California in early December and was in Mrs. Que's fifth-grade class. She's in the chemistry club with all of us.

"At my old school," explained Tala, "we had a trip canceled to Gold Rush country outside of Sacramento because we didn't have enough chaperones. We couldn't even reschedule it. I was so sad, because you get to dress up in old-fashioned clothes and pan for real gold. They tried to make us feel better by a having field trip to the bowling alley and saying it had math applications. But it wasn't the same. So yeah, it can happen."

"Well, maybe in California," stated Elijah. "But not here at Rosalind Franklin Elementary in Michigan."

"Don't worry," I said. "We'll figure it out." I held up my hand. "Scout's honor." I wasn't a Girl Scout now, but I used to be, so I figured the honor oath still held.

"Kate's right," said Birdie. "It will be fine."

"Well, I really want to see tiger sharks," said Memito. He popped a chip into his mouth. "Those dudes will sink their teeth into anything in the water. In their stomachs, fishermen have found license plates, money, cameras. Seriously, they'll eat anything."

"Including you," said Elijah, grinning. "If you lean into the tank too far."

"Nope." Memito waved his spoon in the air like he

30

was stirring an imaginary kettle. "I'd eat those bad boys first. Make myself shark stew with plum tomatoes, cilantro, and onions. Mmm."

"I can't believe you just said that." Phoenix puckered her face. She's been a vegetarian since second grade. "About cooking a shark."

"I can," I said. "Memito eats everything! I really want to see the penguins. They have rockhoppers. My favorite." I smiled just thinking about them.

"Oh, I saw them at the Shedd," said Tala in an excited voice. "They have these little bright yellow feathers on the top of their heads. They're so cute."

"You've already been?" I asked, clearly surprised since she moved to the Midwest about a month and a half ago.

"Yeah," said Tala, who opened up her thermos full of hot soup. A burst of steam shot out. I wasn't completely sure why it did that. Hmm, I'd have to look that up later.

"We went to the Shedd after we were all unpacked after moving here in December," continued Tala. "My family is big into science museums and places like aquariums. Guess what T-shirt I got there?"

"A seahorse," guessed Elijah.

Tala shook her head. And I realized I had no idea since I hadn't known Tala that long. Plus, it was way too cold to be wearing T-shirts in January.

"Hey, I know what shirt you got," said Birdie with a smile. "A starfish. Since you're into astronomy."

"Yes! Only they're officially called sea stars 'cause they're not actually fish," Tala explained.

"When I went, I got the—" started Memito.

"The shark T-shirt," I completed. "We know because we've seen it a bajillion times."

"Yeah," said Memito. "But I also want to get an octopus T-shirt. 'Cause those things are cool. I just wish I had eight arms. I could cook a meal, do my homework, and wash my hair at the same time."

"I have an octopus T-shirt," said Avery.

"It's so soft," said Phoenix. "It's my favorite shirt to borrow when we have impromptu sleepovers."

Elijah drummed his hands on the table. "And I've got a beluga whale one."

"Oh, and Birdie, you have that jelly T-shirt with seaweed," I said.

"Yeah, I love that shirt," said Birdie. "I got it when my cousins from Boston came to town and we went to the aquarium together."

"Hey, I have an idea!" said Avery. "We should all wear our T-shirts to the aquarium."

"That's an awesome idea," said Tala, and everyone nodded.

Everyone except for me, that is. Our family hasn't been to the aquarium in five years. Not since my little brother, Liam, was born. I got a stuffed animal penguin at the time, which was great, and a T-shirt. I've way outgrown it. I have a teddy bear that wears it now.

Everyone was so happy and high-fiving, and I was feeling a little silly about feeling badly. So what? I'd stand out from my friends. No big deal. I tried to shrug it off. I tried to smile along with everyone else. But I guess I'm just not good at keeping my feelings inside. I felt like I was full of gas molecules under pressure. You know, like when you shake up a soda with the cap still on.

So I wasn't that surprised when five minutes later, Birdie asked me, "What's up, Kate?" We were alone and heading to the bathroom, right before we had to be back in the classroom. She nudged my shoulder.

Usually, I try to be positive and not a complainer.

But there was no way I was going to hold back from my best friend.

"I don't have a shirt. Well, one that fits," I admitted. "You know, from the aquarium. It's seriously not a big deal. But . . ." My words trailed off.

Birdie gave me a hug by the water fountain. "You're feeling left out."

"Yeah." I shrugged. "Maybe, kinda, sorta." Why was I getting emotional about this? It was just a dumb T-shirt. "Wait. I think I have a plan." Then I leaned over and told Birdie all about it.

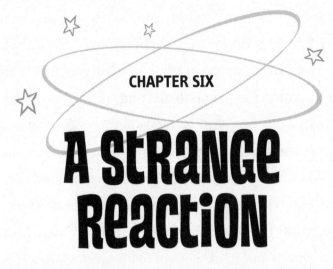

CHAPTER SIX

A STRANGE REACTION

Exchange Reaction (noun). This is a chemical reaction where material gets broken down and put back together. It would be like one kid building a new castle out of blocks while his brother was kicking the old one down.

DOWNSTAIRS, I PLOPPED in front of the family computer. It was Friday afternoon, and my parents let me spend a little more time on the computer during the weekend. The first thing I did was to look up why the steam from Tala's soup burst

out of her thermos. I found out that was because water vapor condensed in the cooler air. I peered out my window to think about what I had just learned. The water vapor must behave more like clouds than smoke. And, scientifically speaking, water vapor is different from steam. That's because steam is just water in the gas phase, and you can't actually see it. I could see the cloud above Tala's lunch because it was made up of little droplets of soup. Yum! I thought about how delicious it would be if the clouds in our skies were made from giant vats of chicken soup.

I laughed aloud at my silly thought. It seemed like a Memito idea.

The next thing I did was start my T-shirt plan.

I figured if I ordered a Shedd Aquarium T-shirt before our field trip, then I'd have a shirt just like all of my friends. As I studied the items on the aquarium store site, I noticed something. They didn't have all of the T-shirts from the actual gift shop. They had a really fun shark T-shirt. And a cute beluga whale tee, but no penguin ones. On the website it said that they had a few select items and to visit the aquarium gift shop for a full selection.

Ugh!

I scrolled again, looking at the beluga T-shirt.

It was okay. But it wasn't a cute rockhopper penguin with bright yellow feathers. I guess I'd just have to wait and buy a penguin T-shirt at the aquarium.

I counted my money in my atom bank. I'd been saving for a really loooong time. All my chore money for the entire fall. Forty dollars. That was more than enough money to buy myself a wonderful penguin T-shirt. Plus, I could surprise Liam and buy him a stuffed animal since he likes them so much.

Even though I wouldn't have an aquarium T-shirt right away, I'd have one in less than two weeks. I could live with that. That is, if we had enough chaperones to go to the aquarium. But we would. I was sure of it. Maybe Dad could be our second chaperone. Then we'd just need two more.

From my room, I grabbed Mr. Penguin, my stuffed animal that my parents bought for me at the Shedd when I was little. He's been ripped up and sewn back together a couple of times—my mom even found a new beak for him from

another penguin that she had bought at a garage sale. After all these years, Mr. Penguin was basically the result of a complicated exchange reaction. Where old parts were taken away. And new parts were added.

And then suddenly, I knew exactly what I would do with Mr. Penguin.

At dinner I hid Mr. Penguin behind my back.

"So guess where my class is going in two weeks?" I said in a mysterious voice. "Well, as long as we get enough parents to chaperone."

Mom looked like she was going to say something, so I gave a warning look. "You're not allowed to guess. So the rest of you—guess!"

"A planetarium," said Dad.

"To the moon," said Liam.

"Sure, in our imagination." I giggled. "I'll give you guys a huge clue." Then, with a flourish, I whipped out Mr. Penguin from behind my back.

Liam leaped for it, but I yanked Mr. Penguin away.

"My Spidey sense tells me you're not going to the South Pole," said Dad. "Unless your mom has applied for a *really* large grant. And while I believe your mom can do anything, chartering a plane to take the entire fifth grade to one of the coldest places on Earth might be stretching it just a bit."

"I am pretty good at grant writing." Mom smiled as she chewed her salad.

I held up Mr. Penguin in front of my face and put on a pretend high voice. "So any real guesses?"

"How about the aquarium?" said Dad.

"You got it!" I tossed Mr. Penguin up in the air so he did a complete twirl. "It's going to be awesome. Liam, did you know that there are thirty-two thousand sea creatures there? And not just fish? Also snakes, birds, and even insects."

"Wow. You sound like a brochure," Dad said, biting into his chicken leg.

"Well, we've been learning about it. I mean, you guys know that they have whales. Not every aquarium has that. Belugas, which are sort of like dolphins, only bigger. Plus that Caribbean Reef exhibit with ninety thousand gallons of water. It's got a bonnethead shark, stingrays, and huge fish called tarpons."

"Oh, I remember that exhibit," said Mom. "There

was a sweet green sea turtle in there."

"Yes," I said. "He's still there. His name is Nickel, and they have this diver who will go into the tank and talk to people. I'm so excited to go to the aquarium for a second time."

"Correction," said Mom. "Your third time. Dad and I brought you when Grandpa Jack and Grandma Dort visited from Texas. You were two, and we pushed you around in a stroller. You kept on yelling about the penguins."

Dad shook his head and laughed. "Not much has changed."

"Hey, no fair." Liam slumped back in his chair. "I haven't even gone once." He harrumphed.

"You'll get your chance, Liam," said Mom. "Maybe we'll go this summer. It's just that I'm so busy during the year." Mom looked at Dad, who was glancing down at his phone. "Greg, wouldn't July be perfect?" Midsummer is basically the only time that Mom is actually free. In early and later summer, she has meetings.

Liam grabbed the penguin from me and clutched it to his chest. "Hey, can Snowie be mine again?"

Even though Mr. Penguin was mine, Liam had loved him so much that I said he could borrow him sometimes. And whenever he borrows him, he renames him. I'm fine with that, honestly. I'm not a go-to-bed-with-a-stuffed-animal kind of person anyway.

"So, Dad, I bet you'd like to see all that great stuff at the aquarium," I said enthusiastically. "Plus, it's in Chicago. You could wave hi to the Bulls."

"Well, you can definitely wave for me."

"No, I mean in person. As a chaperone."

"When is it again?" asked Dad.

"Two weeks from today. Say yes, please? The zebra shark is a threatened species. Which means if you don't see it at the Shedd, it'll be hard to see anywhere. And it's a great opportunity to support them. The sharks, I mean." And then I started listing other animals. "Penguins, dolphins, jellies, eels. All of them."

"I got you." Dad bent down his head and examined his schedule on his phone. "I'll be able to tell you in exactly one sec." Then he peered up at me with a look on his face that was both happy and sad at the same time. Which made absolutely no sense.

CHAPTER SEVEN

CONFERENCE TIME

Conference (noun). Scientists and other professionals attend conferences in order to keep up with the latest findings in their field. It's like a giant professional birthday party, only usually there aren't presents. Instead there are present-ers, who speak at the conference.

"I HAVE SOME BAD NEWS and good news," said Dad.

"Can you give me the good news first?" I pleaded.

"Sure. I've been asked to give a talk in Detroit. On the benefits of mindfulness." Dad's a psychologist, so he goes to a conference every few months. He says he does it to keep up with the industry. Dr. Caroline, my favorite chemist on YouTube, does the same thing. Only she goes to chemistry conferences.

42

"That's great, Dad," I said. "About the conference." I had a feeling that him giving a talk wasn't going to be all that great when it came to the aquarium.

"Usually when I go to conferences, it's to get continuing education credits to keep my license current so I can still talk to patients. I haven't done one in a while, and I'm excited about it. But my talk is on the first day of the conference—January 28. And I'll also be on a panel in the morning, which I'm not too thrilled about because I'll have to improvise."

"That's awesome, Dad," I said. "About the talk and the panel." But inside I really wasn't feeling so great. More like lumpier than the mashed potatoes on my plate.

From across the table, Mom was beaming. "I'm so proud of your dad. It's going to be livestreamed, so I'll be able to catch a little bit of it."

"Dad needs a license for his job?" asked Liam. "I thought that was to drive a car."

"It's a different kind of license," said Dad. "It's to be a psychologist. Just like I need a card that says I can drive, I need one that says I can do my job. Teachers need them too. And doctors."

"Oh." Liam patted Mr. Penguin. "How about kids? And penguins? Do they need licenses too?"

"None that I've heard of," said Dad. "But that is a good business idea." Even though Dad loves his work, he jokes he'll make a bundle one day due to some business idea, retire, and then spend the rest of his time reading books and traveling the world.

"I guess you don't need to give me the bad news," I murmured. "Since I can tell you're going to be busy that day."

"Katie Lane, I'm sorry." Katie Lane is my nickname, in honor of Lois Lane from *Superman*. My dad came up with it because I was super curious as a little kid, just like Lois Lane. "I really wish I could go," Dad continued. "I love aquariums. But I agree with Mom. We'll go to the Shedd as a family this summer. And I don't have any conferences coming up this spring, so hit me up for the next field trip. Okay?" Dad folded his hands together and paused. "Honestly, I'm disappointed I can't go with you."

"It's no big deal," I said. "I'm sure plenty of other parents can go. Like Elijah's. It'll be fine."

"I figured," said Dad.

"I certainly hope so," said Mom softly.

A little part of me worried that maybe I wouldn't get my penguin shirt at all. But that was just being silly.

CHAPTER EIGHT

WHAT'S IN THE BAG?

Atoms (noun). Atoms are so teeny-tiny that you can't see them with your eyes or even a regular microscope. Atoms are made up of even smaller particles called electrons, protons, and neutrons. Just like soccer balls, they move due to gravity or because of force.

ON MONDAY, Mrs. Eberlin held up a brown paper bag. "I've got something exciting to share with all of you."

"Brownies?" asked Memito with a hopeful expression.

"A tennis ball," guessed Avery.

I shot up my hand. "Some atoms.

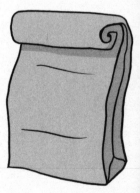

Get it?" I said. "No matter what, that bag is full of atoms and molecules."

Birdie giggled. "I hope those atoms are bonded together into some fun art supplies for us."

Our teacher rustled the bag. "Inside, I have the names of sea creatures. And you're going to pick one to research, and then you're going to present your findings to the class in a five-minute Google Slides presentation. You will offer a description, habitat, diet, behavior, and present status."

Mrs. Eberlin had just taught us about present status. That's the phrase scientists use to describe the current numbers in the world. For rockhopper penguins, their present status is a population of about 1.5 million penguins. And the present status of zebras is about 500,000.

She continued, "The best part is that you will have a super-duper cool facts section. And I want you to discover three of these facts at the aquarium. Something you learn by observing or by asking questions of an animal expert there or by reading something in an exhibit. Your presentation will be two weeks from today, on Monday, January 31. This way when we get to the aquarium you'll already be experts, because you'll have done most of your research." She glanced up at us. "Isn't it wonderful that you get to meet your sea animal in person at the aquarium?"

"That is, if we go," moaned Memito. "We need more chaperones. So far, we just have Avery's dad."

Mrs. Eberlin glanced at the calendar. It was Monday, January 17. "We still have eleven days," she said in an upbeat voice.

"Yay! Plenty of time," I said. "We're going to go. I'm sure of it." I couldn't help feeling that as the principal's daughter, I was somehow extra responsible for stuff. Which is probably ridiculous, but I couldn't help it. Especially since deep down, I wasn't so sure it would all work out.

Folding her hands, Mrs. Eberlin gazed at the entire class. "I sent emails to your parents asking them to look at their schedules. No doubt we'll hear from some more folks soon."

Then she shook the brown paper bag so it crinkled. "It's time to pick your sea creature for your presentation." The first person she walked up to was Birdie.

Birdie reached her hand into the bag and pulled out a folded piece of paper. Slowly, she unwrapped it.

"I'm aging a hundred years," said Jeremy. "Tell us."

"A seahorse," said Birdie softly. I could tell she was a little disappointed. I bet she wanted something more colorful that she could draw.

Next up was Elijah, who pulled out an otter. There was a collective "Ooooh, so cute," and Elijah had a big grin on his face.

Jeremy rubbed his hands together. "I'm going to get a shark. I can feel it. Bring on the predator, bay-bee!" He stirred his arm and pulled out his paper. His face fell. "Parrotfish? Is that a real fish? If it's a bird, then she"—he pointed at Birdie—"should have it." Then he made a *caw-caw* sound like a crow.

"Jeremy," said Mrs. Eberlin. "That's not appropriate. I'm going to have to write your name on the whiteboard." She wrote *Jeremy* in red marker on the section of the board she reserved for people who had strikes against them. Three strikes and you get sent to my mom. Luckily, I have never gotten three strikes. "And that means no recess unless you can show me better behavior."

Jeremy slumped in his seat. "Okaaaay," he

murmured. Outside it was pretty sunny, so there was definitely going to be outdoor recess, which made me feel more than a tiny bit happy.

Next Phoenix got a jellyfish, which seemed to make her smile. And Avery got a shark. Lots of kids whistled for that one, including me.

When it was my turn, I dug my hand in real fast. *Please, please let it be a penguin.* Quickly, I unfolded the paper.

"A sea lion," I said. I tried to keep the disappointment out of my voice. Because I love penguins so much. If I'm ever stressed out, I will watch penguin cams and penguin videos on YouTube.

"Sea lions are so much fun," said Phoenix. "When my family visited San Francisco, we saw them at Fisherman's Wharf. They make a barking sound almost like a dog."

"Nice," I said, still trying to sound upbeat. Then Phoenix started chatting about her family's trip to San Francisco, but it was really hard to pay attention because instead I was looking over at Julia. Julia, who was smiling. Julia, who was waving a slip of paper and going, "I got penguins, you guys!"

She didn't get just any penguins.

She got *my* rockhopper penguins.

"I don't know anything about them," Julia said. "Except they live in the North Pole and they're cute!"

"Actually, they live in the South Pole," I said. "Antarctica, parts of southern Africa, and South America. The only thing in the North Pole is Santa's workshop."

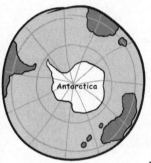

"Oh, cool," said Julia. "Literally. Since it's freezing cold wherever there are penguins."

I bit my lip. Some penguins live at the tip of Africa, where temperatures can be a bit balmy. Even in Antarctica they sometimes have temperatures that are not so freezing during the summer.

When I turned around, I noticed that Birdie was super quiet and slumpy. She looked as disappointed as I was. "You wanted jellies," I said.

"Yeah," she admitted. "I was really looking forward to drawing them for our report. I mean, I like seahorses too. But with jellies I wanted to work on my shading skills and showing how they're translucent and reflect the light."

"Why don't you ask to switch with Phoenix? You know that she loves horses. And seahorses are as close as you can get underwater."

"Kate, that's a great idea!" Birdie went over to Phoenix and asked if she would swap. I couldn't hear Phoenix's response, but she jumped up and hugged Birdie. They exchanged their little pieces of paper, and then Birdie skipped back to her seat.

Now she was suddenly humming and doodling jellies all over her notebook paper. I sighed in a good kind of way. It made me happy to see my friends happy.

Now I just needed to do the same for myself. But when Mrs. Eberlin heard that Birdie and Phoenix had swapped, she said, "Going forward, I'd prefer if the rest of you didn't switch with others."

Mrs. Eberlin didn't say no to swapping. She just said *prefer*. There was a difference, I told myself. As our teacher continued speaking, all I could think about was switching to penguins. Next we did a math lesson, and when we were working in groups on our math sets, I crept over to Julia's table.

"You need to sit down," whispered Julia. Her eyes on Mrs. Eberlin. She looked worried.

"Are you happy with penguins?" I asked.

"Yes."

"Oh. Would you want to switch?"

"I don't think so," she said. "Mrs. Eberlin had a procedure for us choosing our sea creatures. And I wouldn't want to get in trouble."

"Yes, but Birdie and Phoenix swapped and—"

"Didn't you hear? Mrs. Eberlin said she would prefer if we didn't. Now could you please go? I'm checking over my math problems."

"Right," I said. I guessed I could recheck my problems too. But I felt too slumpy.

If my life were a weather forecast, it would be cloudy, gray, and disappointing.

CHAPTER NINE

What's the Matter?

Law of Conservation of Matter (noun). A law that tells us that an amount of matter stays the same even when it changes form. Matter is basically anything with mass that takes up space. That means if you took a bite of your piece of pizza and offered it to your friend, in some sense the amount of matter that made up the slice stays the same. Only now some of that matter is inside your tummy and some of it is in your bestie's!

"BEFORE WE START our math lesson, I want to collect field trip permission slips," said Mrs. Eberlin on Friday, January 21. It was a week before we were going to the Shedd. Some kids opened up their notebooks, while others had to race to their backpacks to get them. Mine was in an envelope that Mom had given me.

"Thanks so much," said Mrs. Eberlin as she set down her mug of coffee. It was so warm I could practically see the steam. And boy, did the air smell good. It made me think of the law of conservation, which states that even if a little bit of the coffee changed from a liquid to gas, the amount of particles didn't change. It's just that some of the water in the coffee had evaporated.

"Remember that the deadline to turn in your signed permission forms is Monday," said Mrs. Eberlin as she went down the aisle collecting permission slips. "Since the entry fee is in the school budget, that part is covered. But if you want anything extra from the gift shop, that will be up to you."

I thought about my forty dollars in my atom bank. Yeah, luckily, I had that part covered.

"Also, I wanted to check on chaperones," continued Mrs. Eberlin. "I reached out to your parents again last night via email, and I know a bunch of your parents were checking their schedules, which is good. As a reminder, we'll need to have our definite list of chaperones set before we go."

She didn't add the *or else.*

But she didn't need to.

Everyone knew that if we didn't find the chaperones really soon, our field trip next Friday could be canceled. But the animal presentation wouldn't. I had been working on my sea lion presentation all week. Honestly, the research was going a little slowly since I had so much to learn. Unlike with penguins, especially rockhoppers, where I knew facts just off the top of my head. For example, I know that rockhoppers are awesome rock climbers because they have sharp claws that help to grip the boulders. So far, I had gotten the information for the habitat and behavior sections for the sea lion as well as the description. I just needed to learn more about their diet and present status.

I had no idea what the present status of sea lions was. Once I solved that mystery, I needed to complete my super-duper facts section, which hopefully would be from actual research at the aquarium, but right now I wasn't so sure.

"Hey, I've got good news," called out Elijah. "My mom can come."

"What? Really?" I said. Since Elijah lives next door

to me, I usually hear everything firsthand. "When did that happen?"

"She told me last night," said Elijah. "She convinced one of the other doctors to cover her shift at the hospital. And another one for the clinic."

"That's wonderful news," said Mrs. Eberlin. "Elijah's mom is a pediatrician. That means we'll have first aid more than covered. Now we just need two more chaperones." She crossed her fingers.

Usually, just like a proton, I'm positive.

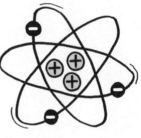

But right now, I was more like an electron. Negative and upset that I couldn't do a penguin presentation.

"At least the weather report is good for the day of our trip," said Mrs. Eberlin. "Cold temps but no snow. For now. It's a long-term forecast and a week away, so anything can happen between now and then. Also, I wanted to remind you all that we're going to leave for the field trip first thing in the morning. So nobody can be late. And we definitely don't want to be late since we've signed up for the eleven o'clock aquarium show, and we don't want to miss that. They change up the animals in the show. But I have heard that ours will be penguins and belugas."

I started to clap. Penguins! That was just awesome. That meant I'd actually be able to get really close to them. The field trip was just a week away, but I already knew that it would be one long week.

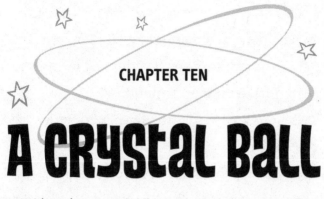

CHAPTER TEN

A CRYSTAL BALL

Crystal (noun). A type of solid made up of molecules and ions arranged in a definite three-dimensional pattern. Salt and sugar are examples of tasty crystals that have their own unique crystal structures.

ON THE OTHER SIDE of the playground, I could hear Julia bossing around some fourth graders. Telling them not to run so they "wouldn't slip on the ice like penguins." She took her job in student government pretty seriously, especially since they have a new safety campaign.

"I just wish I could do my presentation on penguins," I said to Birdie and Tala, who stood by the swings. And I explained how Julia didn't seem to get penguins. I knew that they rarely slipped on ice.

"I don't see why you can't do it too," said Tala. "It's not too late. The presentation's not for ten days."

I shook my head. "Mrs. Eberlin just wants one person per animal for our presentations."

"Sea lions are wonderful, Kate," said Birdie. "I wish you could see that."

"Yeah, but penguins surf through waves, dive off cliffs, and will lie on their bellies and toboggan down a hill. Now, that's fun." I sighed heavily. "I could seriously give my presentation on penguins tomorrow. I mean, I know way more penguin-y things than Julia."

"True," said Birdie. "But wouldn't you have more fun learning something new about sea lions?"

"Plus, it would be kind of unfair if you did penguins," said Tala. "Since you already know so much."

"Wow, it sounds like you guys aren't on my side," I said, hurt.

Birdie's eyes got big. And she looked at Tala anxiously. "No, that's not it at all," said Birdie. "We're just trying to look at the bright side." She scooped up some old snow on the ground and packed it into a ball. Then jokingly said, "Looking

into this crystal ball, I see good things in your future."

"Ha-ha," I said.

"We want you to feel good about your presentation," said Tala.

And then I just stood there not really looking at anything. To me, it seemed unfair that Birdie could talk about this when she and Phoenix got to switch and I didn't. Plus, I bet that Julia didn't have a penguin poster in her room or a penguin stuffed animal that she gave to her little brother. She didn't even have a little brother.

I sighed again.

"I think you need some cheering up," said Birdie.

"Yes," said Tala. "Kate does need some cheering up."

"It's time for Operation Cheer Up Kate. And I think that involves chocolate."

"Definitely chocolate." From watching Dr. Caroline on YouTube, I know that there are six different forms of chocolate crystals that are smooth and glossy and will melt in your mouth. Yum!

"You guys are so right," said Tala. "You should come over to my house after school and we can make snacks for the trip." I smiled really big, since Tala's class was also going on the field trip and on the same bus. "We can make homemade chocolate-covered pretzels," added Tala.

"Oh, that sounds like so much fun!" I cried. "How about if we come to my house though? My dad's working in his office. He likes it if I'm home to keep an eye on Liam."

"Kate's house it is," said Tala. "Will this afternoon work?"

"Yes!" I shouted.

We all joined hands, or rather mittens, and spun in a circle. And then when we broke away, we spun some more.

When the bell rang, Birdie and I raced inside, but then stopped to wait for Tala to catch up. Since she was new to the snow, she had too many layers of clothing on, and took forever to change out of her snow gear.

Jeremy called out, "Tala looks like a penguin."

"Be quiet, Jeremy," I said. And I gritted my teeth.

It seemed like everyone and everything wanted to remind me of penguins.

CHAPTER ELEVEN

OPEN UP!

Objectivity (noun). Discovering the best explanation by allowing evidence—not bias—to answer the question. In science, it's considered a bias when scientists come to incorrect conclusions based on false data. Sort of like your little brother telling you that your dog ate your chocolate chip cookie and you believing him—when in fact, your brother actually snarfed down your cookie.

"IS THERE ANYTHING you'd like to talk about, Kate?" asked Dad. I was pacing by the front door, waiting for Tala and Birdie to arrive with the ingredients for Operation Cheer Up Kate. "You seem upset."

We were planning on making chocolate-covered pretzels. Some to eat now and some to pass around as snacks for the field trip on Friday. We needed to make over one hundred so there would be enough for everyone in both fifth-grade classes to have a couple.

"Um, not really." I continued to pace.

"Kate," he said in a gentle reprimand. My dad knew me so well. Plus, he's a psychologist. So then I told him how I was still upset about not getting penguins as my topic for my sea animal presentation. How having to do sea lions just didn't seem as much fun.

"You're biased and not being objective," said Dad. "Why don't you focus on making new discoveries about sea lions? You're a curious person. You might surprise yourself. It's good to go outside your comfort zone."

"It's not about comfort, Dad. It's about love. You and Mom are the ones who tell me you should pursue what your passions are."

"Yes, but there are many paths to take and many lessons to learn. And—"

"If you think it's important to go outside your comfort zone, why are you upset about being on the panel for your conference?"

"Oh, you've got me there." He smiled with a guilty look. "Maybe it's something we both need to work on, huh, Katie Lane?"

Then his phone buzzed in his pocket. "Oh,

speaking of the conference." He glanced down at his phone. "That's one of the conference organizers." Then he walked into his office, just as Birdie and Tala burst into the house, carrying a shopping bag full of supplies. Thirty minutes later, Tala, Birdie, and I stood in my kitchen making our chocolate-covered pretzels.

"We definitely will have more than enough for our field trip to the aquarium," said Tala. She pointed at all the pretzel rods we had already dipped in chocolate. It had been Birdie's idea to decorate them with rainbow sprinkles.

"To make them pizzazz-y for our trip," said Birdie.

Soon enough, Liam was in the kitchen begging us to take him with us so he could see the aquarium and eat chocolate pretzel snacks.

He clasped his small hands together. "I want to go. Please. Please. Please take me with you! I'll squish into your backpack."

"Oh, I wish you could go," I said. "But, buddy, it's just for fifth graders."

Liam sighed heavily. "No fair. How come old kids get to have all the fun?" He still looked disappointed, along with Dribble, our dog. Who was pitifully begging with his eyes all big and his tongue lolling.

"Here," I said, handing Liam a pretzel. "This will cheer you up."

"Thanks," he said, biting into it. "It's yummy!" Then he took off for the family room, with a hopeful Dribble at his heels.

Forty-five minutes later, we almost had all of the pretzels dipped into chocolate. Except for the ones we were dipping in white chocolate.

I broke up the white chocolate into small, bite-sized pieces, and then I put them into the glass bowl. Next Birdie dumped in three tablespoons of vegetable shortening. "This stuff is so icky looking."

"Yeah, but you need it," I said. "Anyway, it melts, so you can't tell it's there."

After popping the bowl into the microwave, I checked the chocolate. It looked nice and creamy.

I was just about to start dipping again when there was a knock on the door. Dribble started barking. "Calm down," I told him.

"Maybe it's someone delivering a package," said Tala.

"No chance," I said. "My parents are on a break from ordering stuff online. They want to support local businesses this month." Dribble followed me to the door, his tail wagging.

It was Elijah with Memito and Jeremy too.

"Hey," I said. "What's up?"

"Well, the guys were just hanging out when we had this idea," said Elijah.

I let them into the house. "It's Elijah," I called out.

"And Memito," said Memito.

"And Jeremy," said Jeremy.

The boys waltzed into the kitchen. Immediately, Memito beelined for the tray of pretzels.

"Sorry, you'll have to wait," I said.

"Until the field trip," chorused Birdie and Tala.

"About that," said Elijah. "We have something to tell you. It's that—"

"Technically, white chocolate isn't real chocolate," said Memito. "Because it doesn't have any cocoa solids. It's made from sugar, cocoa butter, milk stuff, and vanilla."

"Let me see." Jeremy stuck his fingers into the chocolate mixture. "Tastes good! I don't care about technical stuff."

"Hey, stop that," I said. "You just spread your germs everywhere." Jeremy could be so infuriating.

"But I just washed my hands," said Jeremy. "With mud and oil and decaying stuff from the garbage."

Tala scrunched up her face and plugged her nose like she could smell the stink.

"He's just kidding," said Elijah. "His hands are clean. My mom makes him sanitize before stepping into our house." Elijah's mom, the doctor, is super serious about everything being clean.

I put my hands on my hips. "So, did you guys seriously come here to tell us that white chocolate isn't real chocolate?"

Memito looked at Elijah, and Elijah looked at Jeremy, who shrugged. "Actually, we're here because we had this idea," Elijah said, resting his elbow on the counter. Immediately, it slid out from underneath him and he lost his balance, toppling into Birdie. She tried to catch him, but her arms were full with the bowl of melted white chocolate. Before we knew it, the two of them were in a pile on the floor, and the white chocolate was everywhere. It was dead silent for a nanosecond before we all burst into laughter.

Through giggles, Elijah asked, "Hey! What did you put on there? Grease?"

"Um, yeah. It's called vegetable shortening," said Memito, who was laughing so hard he could barely help Birdie up.

"Can you please just tell us your plan?" I begged Elijah. Although he could barely understand me because I couldn't stop laughing at my two best friends covered in chocolate.

Eventually Elijah pulled it together enough to explain why they stopped by in the first place. "I thought we could ask your dad to go on the field trip," said Elijah. "He's a psychologist, right? And so he can just reschedule with his patients or find someone to cover for him. Like my mom did."

"I think it's a wonderful idea," I said. "Except for one thing. I already asked him." And then I explained how my dad had a conference where he was speaking.

"Oh, man. Tell him he can speak from the aquarium. You know, go remote on location from a shark tank or something."

"Sure, that would be professional." I rolled my eyes.

"Maybe someone's big brother or sister could come as a chaperone," said Birdie.

Tala shook her head. "They have school too. I don't think my brother who's a freshman in high school could miss algebra to go to an aquarium."

"He could if he had a cool teacher," said Jeremy.

"Even teachers have to stay in school," said Birdie. "The only people who aren't in school or working are retired people."

"Birdie," I said. "You're a genius! I just figured out who we should ask next."

I turned to Memito. "It doesn't have to be a parent, just an adult! What about your grandma? She's retired, right?"

Memito shrugged. "Sure. We can ask her. There's a chance she'll say no, but it can't hurt."

"It's still an awesome idea," said Jeremy. I lifted my eyebrows. I couldn't believe Jeremy thought something I said was awesome. That might be a first.

"We should all go to my house together," said Memito. "I think she would have a harder time saying no to all of us."

We cleaned up the chocolate mess and then ran

to Memito's house. It took us about ten minutes to get there, but it felt like ten hours. Normally, when there's no snow anywhere, it's faster. But we had to go slow on parts of the sidewalk that were a little icy.

"Okay, everyone," I said, "cross your fingers." I lifted my hand to knock.

"Um, Kate," said Memito. "This my house. We don't need to knock."

I laughed. "I sort of forgot," I admitted. Memito led us into his house. We pulled off our boots and coats, and then we made our way to the family room, where Memito's grandma was reading a mystery. We were not surprised to find her wrapped in one of her big quilts, completely focused on her novel.

She jumped when she saw us. "Sorry. In the story the detective was hunting down a notorious group of jewelry thieves. And then I heard this *crunch-crunching* sound."

Memito explained that we were an organized group of high-tech jewelry thieves and that we needed a chaperone to go to the Shedd Aquarium in Chicago.

Chuckling, his grandmother put her reading glasses on the table. "I love that aquarium. Sign me up!"

We all cheered. Sometimes things do go in your favor.

CHAPTER TWELVE

PResent
youR PoiNt

Scientific Presentation (noun). This is when scientists go to conferences and communicate their findings. Usually, this is done by giving a presentation with a visual slideshow. It's always a good idea to know how to present or persuade others of your position. As a kid, sometimes you need to present the reasons why you absolutely need that new rock polisher or chemistry set.

"YOU'RE GOING TO WORK on your presentations today in class," said Mrs. Eberlin. It was Tuesday, three days before we were supposed to go on the field trip. "I want you all to have your research done before we even cross our state line. Think about how much better your experience will be when you finally meet your animal at the aquarium."

"You mean *if* we meet our animal at the aquarium," said Memito. Earlier that morning he had shared the good news about his grandma being able to go. "We're still one chaperone short though."

"After school, I'm going to talk to the principal and figure this out," said Mrs. Eberlin.

I could feel eyes on me. And my face became beet red. You'd think I'd get used to hearing teachers and kids mention the principal. But I never do. It always makes me feel a little awkward and uncomfortable.

"We can solve this," said Mrs. Eberlin. "Now let's focus back on your presentations. You've all been working so hard on your research, I can't wait to hear all of the information you've gathered."

I tried to be happy about focusing on my sea lion talk. After all, it's important for me to practice giving oral presentations. Since that's what scientists often do when they go to conferences. I tried to focus on how lucky I was to get to work on my very own presentation.

But as Mrs. Eberlin passed out our Chromebooks, I kept on worrying about the field trip.

Usually, everyone gets really excited whenever we get to work on something cool like slides. But today, everyone was sluggish and slow. I guess they were as worried as me.

"Oh, I wanted to say something about the photographs for your presentations," said Mrs. Eberlin. "It's okay to cut and paste them on your slides. But you can only use Creative Commons images. I'll show you how to do that in a moment. However, I would encourage all of you to consider making original drawings as well."

"I'm definitely making drawings," said Birdie.

"Same with me," said Julia. "I want to make my penguins magenta. I think that will look cute."

Magenta. There were no such things as magenta penguins.

"Violet would be good too," Julia said.

"Penguins are black and white," I said quietly. "It helps disguise them from predators when they're swimming. Although some also have yellow, orange, and slate blue colors. But not magenta."

"But magenta is cheerful," said Julia, "and it sounds good too. Purple penguins." She smiled.

"It's not scientifically accurate," I explained. Was

74

she serious? Yes, they have orange beaks and cute yellow tufts on their heads, but nowhere on planet Earth are there *magenta* penguins.

"Kate," said Mrs. Eberlin in her perfectly mastered teacher voice. "We're now working on putting headings on our slides in the seven different sections of our reports. Do you remember what order to put them in?"

"Um, kind of." I shrugged.

"I don't think you do, because you weren't paying attention." She glanced across the room. "Avery, can you tell Kate what they are?"

"Sure," said Avery. "Overview. Description. Habitat. Diet and behavior. Plus, present status."

"Okay, I knew that," I said in a quiet voice. "And the three super-duper facts we learn at the aquarium."

"I hope I find out that magenta penguins are real," said Julia. "At the aquarium, that is."

I started twitching in my seat. And gritting my teeth. Birdie gave me a warning look.

I wanted to yell at Julia that if she had already done her research, she would know that there are no purple penguins at the Shedd Aquarium.

But I knew that wouldn't be a smart choice.

Instead, I remembered what my dad taught me to do when trying to make wise choices. I closed my eyes and took three very slow, very deep breaths. That always made me feel better.

I started working on my slides, along with everyone else. I looked up more facts about sea lions for my behavior section and found out that sea lions can dive and stay underwater. Sometimes for up to twenty minutes! They just have to exhale first before they dive below the water's surface. I thought about how cool it would be to swim around the bottom of the ocean for twenty beautiful, uninterrupted minutes.

Mom says she always gets fresh new thoughts whenever she's around the water. That's why we go to Lake Michigan whenever she has free time in the summer.

But my thoughts weren't refreshing. They were just staying on the same worry that I'd had for the past two weeks.

"How will we find our three super-duper facts from the aquarium if we don't go?" I asked Mrs. Eberlin. "What if we don't get our chaperones?"

"Well, Kate," said Mrs. Eberlin. "I have confidence that we'll figure out the chaperone issue."

"Couldn't we just go with three chaperones?" asked Avery.

"I'm afraid not," said Mrs. Eberlin. "Those are our school rules."

"A lot of good it does to have the principal's daughter in our class," moaned Jeremy.

"Wait. It's just about lunchtime. I could ask my mom right now." Everyone turned to look at me. "Maybe I could ask my mom to get a staff person who doesn't need a substitute. Like one of our library clerks or office assistants?"

"Yes, that was my plan," said Mrs. Eberlin. "Great minds think alike."

"Let me ask her now," I said. "I know exactly where she takes her lunch. I'm sure she will say yes."

Everyone looked at me with hopeful eyes. When Mrs. Eberlin handed me a pass to go to the office, I crossed my fingers and said a silent prayer.

Hurrying down the hall to the office, I thought very positive thoughts. Then as I rounded the corner, I smacked into something very solid.

Well, not something.

Someone. An official-looking somebody with a walkie-talkie crackling on her hip. That somebody was the principal, Terri Crawford.

My mother.

"Mom!" I said, glancing up at her. "Oh, I'm sorry for bumping into you. I wasn't looking and—what are you doing here?" Not that I really should have been surprised. After all, she runs Rosalind Franklin Elementary School.

"Honey," she said. "I just was going to see you."

"That's funny. I was just going to find you." Immediately, I asked if our class could have three chaperones instead of four. And she immediately responded that it "wouldn't work."

Then I told her about my idea of using a staff member who didn't need a sub. And how Mrs. Eberlin had the same idea. "Say yes, please, Mom. I think it makes a lot of sense."

"It does. I really like how much thought you've put into this. But the answer is, again, no. I'm not going to have a staff member go on the trip."

I swallowed hard. "Mom, *please*. C'mon, I—"

Mom held up her hand and smiled. "Stop right there. The reason that a staff member isn't going is because *I'm* going on the field trip on Friday."

"What? You . . . but . . . who's going to run the school?"

"I've been working on it for a couple of weeks. Since, as you know, I don't have an assistant principal. But there are larger schools in the district that do. And one of them across town is going to come and help run things on Friday. We just had to get it all cleared at the district level. I wanted to tell you sooner. Much sooner. But I was worried that it might not work out. You see, I came up with the idea that night when you asked Dad. I almost told you about it then. But I had to figure it out first and . . ." She sighed. "Anyway, I'm just so happy it all worked out!"

"Me too, Mom. That's awesome." And then in the middle of the hallway, next to the water fountain, I gave her the most giant hug. Because right in that moment she wasn't Mrs. Crawford, principal. She was just my loving mom. I couldn't wait to race back to the class to tell everyone the amazing news!

CHAPTER THIRTEEN

CHANCES ARE...

Statistics (noun). This is the science of data. Data is the info you get from gathering, observing, and testing an experiment. Data allows scientists to analyze their findings and come up with new conclusions. This is what people mean when they say *run the numbers*. They don't actually mean that numbers need to sprint down a field.

"YOU GUYS! We can go to the aquarium," I shouted as soon as I was back in the classroom. My mom didn't come with me—she had gotten called away on some principal business.

"That's just fantastic," said Mrs. Eberlin. "Is she going to send a library aide?"

I shook my head. "She's coming herself," I said. I'd been so excited that we could go on the field trip that

I'd forgotten the principal was going to go with us. Just what the kids in my class didn't want. I swallowed hard.

"Wait a minute, that means the principal is coming?" Jeremy rolled his eyes. "So we can't do anything wrong." He moaned.

"I don't think it matters if the principal is there or not," said Julia. "You should never be doing things wrong."

"It will be kind of different," admitted Rory Workman.

"Will she wear her name tag?" asked Jeremy.

"Has she ever gone on a field trip before?" asked someone from the back. I didn't turn around. I couldn't. I knew for a fact she definitely hadn't.

It felt like all of my excitement had deflated like a balloon with a hole in it.

"Hey, you guys," said Birdie. "It's awesome that Kate's mom is going. It's seriously way better than not going to the aquarium at all. Anyway, she's really nice."

"Yeah," said Elijah. "She's honestly a lot of fun. You should have seen the scavenger hunt she came up with this summer or the time she made dry ice bubbles with Kate."

"We should feel lucky," said Phoenix. "Because now we're definitely going to the aquarium on Friday."

"Unless it snows," said Memito. "There's a thirty percent chance."

"Well, it sounds like the chance is in our favor," said Elijah.

"What if there's bad weather?" asked Julia, which was suddenly what I was thinking too. "You know, on the day of the aquarium."

"If there's a really bad storm and the school district closes schools, we obviously can't go," said Mrs. Eberlin.

There was a groan. I took a big gulp of air and thought about how the chances were in our favor. Scientists always look at statistics—numbers that communicate their findings—in order to come to the best conclusion.

"But this is Michigan," continued Mrs. Eberlin. "We know how to clear up snow, so let's not worry about that." She peered around the classroom with a serious expression. "Okay, over the next few nights, I want everyone to get some good sleep. And keep working on your projects. So you can be prepared to meet your sea creature in three days."

And then suddenly everyone was cheering, me loudest of all.

CHAPTER FOURTEEN

SOMETHING STINKS

Bacteria (noun). These are one-celled organisms that are also called germs. They exchange chemical signals in order to communicate and attack healthy cells. So next time you use soap, you might be interrupting bacteria having a conversation.

"SEA LIONS SURE KNOW how to have fun," I said. "For one, they like to bodysurf."

On Thursday, at the dinner table, I was reporting some of my sea lion research to my family. I guess it was a way to practice my presentation, which was just about done. Well, all except for the three super-duper facts I'd find at the aquarium tomorrow. I could hardly wait.

"I want to learn to surf," declared Liam.

"Me too," said Mom.

Dad set down his water glass. "Not for me, thank you. I remember one summer during college my buddy and I took a trip out to California. And we saw sea lions swimming not too far from the surfers." He scratched his head. "I wonder if I still have those photos somewhere."

"I want to see the photos," said Liam. He hopped out of his chair and spread out his arms like he was riding a huge wave. "I'm a surfing seal."

"Sea lion," I corrected. "Seals and sea lions are different. Sea lions have ear flaps. Plus, their flippers can rotate under them and they can walk on land. Seals can only sort of slither."

"See, Kate, you really are learning quite a bit about sea lions," said Dad.

"Arfff!" said Liam. He clapped his flippers together. "Arrf."

"Okay, Mr. Sea Lion," said Mom. "It's dinnertime. Come and eat your salmon." She glanced at his empty seat.

Liam climbed back into his seat. "Yuck," he said,

staring at the pink fillet. "I guess I can't be a sea lion after all. Fish is yucky."

"You like salmon, you just forgot," said Mom. "And you love fish sticks."

Dad grabbed the ketchup bottle and poured a blob next to his potatoes and on top of his salmon. "This will disguise the fish taste."

"Not you too." Mom shook her head.

"Just don't want to have fish breath for my panel and talk tomorrow," joked Dad. "Ketchup breath is better."

Both Liam and I giggled as Mom calmly explained how there was no way to have fish breath overnight. Then I remembered how I once watched a Dr. Caroline video on bad breath. When you wake up in the morning, you have billions of bacteria in your mouth. They take in food and excrete waste. The waste—some of it in the form of gas—is what makes your breath stinky. "Just remember to brush your teeth tonight, Dad. Extra long. Good luck at your conference tomorrow," I said.

"And have fun on your trip to the aquarium," said Dad.

Liam stared down at his food. "I still don't see why I can't come with you."

"Because you can't miss school, silly," I said. "But you'll have a chance to go." I looked anxiously up at my parents. "Right?"

Dad popped a potato in his mouth. "Definitely. It will be a whole family thing."

"This summer," added Mom.

"That's a hundred million months away," said Liam.

"Six months, kiddo," said Mom.

"We'll have to work on your math skills," I added. And then reminded him that there was ice cream for dessert. Liam started to smile a little.

And I knew what would get him to smile even more.

After dinner, I counted the money in my atom bank. Yup, I still had my forty dollars. Then I went on the computer to recheck prices at the aquarium gift shop. It looked like I had just enough for a shirt for me and a stuffed animal for Liam. I couldn't wait to surprise him with the gift.

But at that very moment, Liam popped into the family room. He peered right over my shoulder. "Hey," he said. "What's that?" And he pointed at a group of stuffed animals on the screen.

"They're cephalopods," I explained. "The first one is a squid, which you can tell by its elongated body with eight arms and two tentacles. The one in the middle that looks like an underwater elephant is called a cuttlefish. Ms. Daly, our chemistry club advisor, calls them cuttles. And you already know the last one, the octopus. It looks kind of like a squid, with eight arms, but it doesn't have any tentacles. Plus, the octopus's arms are way more flexible. They all belong to the cephalopod family because they have three hearts and squirt ink to defend themselves against predators."

"That's cool." Liam grabbed the pen next to my notebook and uncapped it. "But the arms and the tentacles look the same."

"Yeah, it's hard to tell, but if you look really closely, you can see the difference. Tentacles have suction cups only at the ends of their limbs, whereas arms have suction cups all over," I said, looking over at Liam. "What are you doing?"

"Nothing."

"Don't even think about squirting it. You're not a

cephalopod. Plus," I added, looking around the room, "I don't see any predators."

His eyes shifted over to the money from the atom bank and then back to the screen. "Are you buying one of those stuffed animals?"

"I might be," I said, giving him a wink.

"For someone you know?"

"There's a good possibility."

"Someone you know super-duper well? So well you might be related?"

"That's entirely possible."

"And does his name start with an *L*?"

"That just so happens to be one of my favorite letters in the alphabet."

"Mine too." Now Liam was jumping up and hugging my legs.

"I just can't tell this person who I know super-duper well and whose name starts with an *L* because it's a surprise. So don't say anything."

"I won't," said Liam. "I promise with eight arms and three hearts. 'Cause I'm an octopus." He waved around his arms like he was underwater.

Then he raced away upstairs, singing to himself,

"I'm Octopus Boy." And I knew that I couldn't wait to "surprise" my little brother with my gift.

Then my eyes slid back to my computer screen. And I checked the weather. And saw a giant snowflake next to the forecast. Which meant only one thing.

Snow.

CHAPTER FIFTEEN

DON't Let It SNOW

Snow (noun). It starts in the clouds when the temperature is lower than 0°C, and then the water vapor turns into ice by going directly from a gas to a solid. Basically, it skips the whole liquid stage (as in rain). It's sort of like skipping ahead a grade in school.

NOT ONLY WAS IT supposed to snow tomorrow, there was supposed to be a lot of it. I spun around the room, thinking of everything I knew about snow.

First off, it needs to be cold.

Check.

It was going to be exactly freezing tomorrow. As in all day. That's 0°C or 32°F.

And for snow to form, there has to be dirt. Not here on Earth's surface, but up there in the sky. I learned about that from Dr. Caroline. Basically, snow happens when ice crystals form around specks of dirt that are floating in the air. When all of these crystal dirt particles collide, they stick together. And then they get bigger and bigger until—*bam!*—they get so heavy they plop down to Earth.

And fall on your head.

As snowflakes.

And there wasn't anything that I could do to stop that from happening.

Not unless I got a giant leaf blower or something and I could blow all of the little specks of dirt out of the sky.

Then I remembered something else that I had learned from Dr. Caroline. How salt can lower the freezing point of water. So maybe if I sprinkled it on our sidewalk, driveway, and cul-de-sac, the snow would just melt. Mom had gone back to school after dinner, trying to clear out her work, so I raced over to my dad's workbench, which was in the basement.

I sprinted down the stairs. "Dad! I've got to talk to you. It's an emergency."

Dad told me to stand behind the black tape that marked off the safe zone. He put it down last year after Liam wandered too close to the table saw. Luckily, Dad was paying attention and no one got hurt, but we had to have a big family meeting to talk about safety.

He handed me a pair of safety goggles and asked me about the emergency. I told him about how it was supposed to snow. And how it might be hard to get the car out of the driveway in order to go to school to meet the bus for the field trip.

But then I told him about my salt plan.

We live on a cul-de-sac at the back of our neighborhood, and the plows don't get there sometimes until later. So even though school could be open, it could be challenging to get out of the neighborhood.

"I like the way you're thinking, Kate," he said. "But first of all, the weather report doesn't say a hundred percent chance of snow. It's now only at fifty-five percent, so it could go either way. Second of all, we'd need many bags of rock salt to do the job. And I just have one bag in the garage. Even if we could borrow another bag from Elijah's family, two bags wouldn't cut it." He sighed deeply. "Third of all, the salt may prevent ice from forming, but it's not going to stop the snow from falling. We've got snow tires on our cars, though, so if school isn't canceled, we should still be able to get there."

I thought about that. "True, and we could even walk to the school bus if we had to," I said. That's because there's a bus stop on Maple Avenue, which always gets plowed, about five blocks away.

"The only problem is that the morning school bus can only take kids as passengers."

"Essh." That meant Elijah's mom, our much-needed chaperone, and my mom technically couldn't get on board. And even if my mom could pull some strings as principal, Elijah's mom couldn't, and we needed every single chaperone.

"Well, there's no point in salting the street until after the plow has come through. But we can certainly shovel the sidewalk and the driveway, and then salt the ground to keep it from icing over. We have enough salt for that."

That's when Liam raced down the stairs, into the basement. "Shoveling? Who's shoveling? I want to shovel!"

"You can, Liam," said Dad.

"Well," I said, looking outside at the fat milky-white clouds, "you'll have to wait until it snows first."

"And since there's only a fifty-five percent chance," Dad added, "it might not."

Liam looked at me. "I want to shovel. And I want it to snow. But I also want you to be able to go to the aquarium, Kate."

"And don't forget Dad's conference," I said.

"Yeah, that too."

I looked outside once again, and at the forecast. "Looks like we'll just have to wait and see."

There was just one little problem. Waiting is my least favorite activity.

CHAPTER SIXTEEN

PLOWING THROUGH

Freezing Point (noun). This is the temperature where a liquid becomes a solid. For water, the freezing point is 0°C or 32°F. But for gasoline it has to be a lot colder. At least -40°C. That's why it's possible to drive around in cold climates and not have the fuel tank in your car turn into an ice cube. Although an ice cube derby sounds like a lot of fun!

THURSDAY NIGHT WAS the longest night ever. I barely got any sleep because I kept jolting awake thinking it was time for the field trip.

At 2:00 a.m. it was definitely not time.

Or at 3:00 a.m. when I was woken up by snowplows roaring in the distance.

But at 4:30 a.m. it was time. Still early, but more "morning" than "middle of the night" at least.

I jumped out of bed and looked out the window. It was dark outside, but I could still see. That's because there was snow on the ground. A lot of it.

But I could tell by looking at the streetlight that it had stopped coming down. Well, except for one or two stray snowflakes. That was a good sign. After getting dressed, I put on all my snow gear—snow pants, winter coat, scarf, hat, boots, two layers of gloves, and my face mask for really cold weather. Turning on the lights, I could see that my parents had left their cars in our driveway. Mom had the SUV, and Dad had his sedan. The SUV wouldn't have a problem backing out. But today, Dad was taking the SUV to Detroit and Mom was driving the sedan to school.

There was no way she could back out without getting stuck. The snow was too deep. Unless we shoveled the entire driveway. And not only the driveway. The street.

The snowplow would get to our part of the

neighborhood eventually, but who knew when that would happen?

We couldn't wait.

Even if Mom could get out of our driveway, it would be hard for her to drive to Maple Avenue, which would be all nice and plowed.

Normally, we could get a ride with Elijah's mom. Only we couldn't this morning. Their car was in the shop. And they were planning on getting a ride with us.

So I got to work. After I had cleared the walkway leading up to the house, Mom and Dad trundled outside with Liam. "Great job shoveling the path," said Dad. "That's my girl."

"Thanks, Dad."

Then I asked Mom the question I didn't want to ask. "Do you think school is canceled?"

She bit her bottom lip. "Well, actually, funny you should ask."

"Good funny?"

"Funny in that I just got a message. And school is on."

"Yeah!" I shouted.

Liam did too. "That means I'll be getting my octo—"

"Shhh," I said. "That part's a surprise." I looked at our long driveway and tried not to panic. How were we going to get rid of all this snow?

While I helped my mom start to shovel the driveway, Liam raced away and came back a few minutes later with a saltshaker.

"Thanks, Liam," I said. "But remember how Dad said that we need to wait until the plow goes through before spreading the salt?"

"Besides, I don't think you have enough," said Mom.

"Oh, man," said Liam. "What are you going to do?"

I glanced at the spot where our outdoor water spigot was buried in snow. And I suddenly came up with a plan.

"Hey! Where are you going?" Liam called after me as I glided away on the ice.

"You'll see," I said. First thing I did was grab a coiled-up garden hose from our shed. Then I carried it into the garage and plopped in front of the utility sink. Then I turned on the faucet until the water got nice and hot. When you have warm water, the molecules zip around super quick. I wanted to get the water molecules on our driveway moving as fast as possible so that the snow would melt into liquid water.

I turned off the water for a minute while I attached the hose to the spigot and stretched the hose out the side door. Then I pushed down on the spray nozzle and aimed the stream of water onto the driveway.

Yes, those molecules must really have been zipping along, because the snow got lumpier and lumpier until it melted. My family watched in wonder.

"That's so cool!" shouted Liam.

"I wish I had thought of it years ago," said Mom.

"And we're lucky it's not too cold out," added Dad.

My hand hurt from squeezing so hard, but I was grinning. You could see most of the asphalt. And Dad was right about it not being that cold. Because if the ground was still frozen, then the hot water would soon become cold water and just freeze up. Luckily, the temperature was hovering just above freezing, so hopefully we would be okay. I crossed my fingers just in case.

"I could always drop you guys off in the SUV," said Dad as he climbed into the driver's seat.

Mom shook her head. "You need to leave now,

honey, if you want to make it to Detroit in time. And we still have stuff to get ready for the field trip."

Dad looked reluctant as he backed his way out the driveway. The SUV slowly made its way down our street onto the wider avenue.

Once Dad was out of sight, we turned our attention back to the driveway. There were still a few patches of thick ice, so I found a bag of leftover sand from Liam's old sandbox and spread that around. The sand would add traction. Plus, it also prevents ice from forming. That's because the movement of the grains of sand messes with the ability of water molecules to cling together and make ice. And we definitely did not need any more ice.

After thirty minutes of carrying sand back and forth from the garage, we had finally created a path for Mom's car to get out of the long driveway.

But there was just one problem. What about navigating the unplowed street? The sedan didn't have the traction of the SUV, and we were completely out of sand. Back inside the house, I got ready for school, and then out the window the most amazing thing happened—I could see a snowplow clearing the street. We would be able to get to school!

Making sure to tuck my money into the safest pocket of my backpack, I did Tala's happy dance. We were going to the aquarium, and I was going to meet sea lions and rockhopper penguins. This was going to be the best field trip ever!

CHAPTER SEVENTEEN

A WONDERLAND

Sodium (noun). This is a chemical element that is a silvery-white metal. When combined with the element chlorine, it can form a crystal known as sodium chloride, otherwise known as salt. Next time you want more salt on your fries, ask for sodium chloride, and you'll sound like a hungry scientist.

"IT'S BEAUTIFUL, ISN'T IT?" asked Birdie. We stood in line in the pickup circle in front of the school. The whole world was covered in fresh snow. The white on the boughs of the pine trees made them look even greener somehow. And the sun shone through a patch of clouds, making everything sparkle.

"It is!" I clapped my mittens together, staring at the bus. "Look at it. Just waiting for us. All shiny and yellow."

Birdie whipped around. "I meant that snow." She giggled.

"I meant the bus," I said, "because it's taking us to the aquarium."

"I know," said Birdie. She pulled out her bag of ginger chews. "See, I'm prepared. And wearing this." She unzipped her coat to show me her long-sleeve jellyfish shirt. I knew that Tala had her sea star shirt on, just like Memito had his shark shirt. Avery had on her octopus shirt, and Elijah was wearing his beluga shirt. Soon enough, I'd get my penguin shirt at the aquarium. I smiled at the thought.

A couple minutes later, Mrs. Eberlin said we had to get organized into our field trip groups. She held a clipboard and started to call out names of the kids who would go with chaperones. "Some of you will go with chaperones from Mrs. Que's class and some from mine. Just listen up as we call your name, and you'll hear who your chaperone is going to be." Elijah's mom got Mia Wong, Skyler, and three kids from Mrs. Que's class, two with nut allergies and one with epilepsy. Since she's a pediatrician, she would know what to do in case of an emergency.

Memito went to stand by his grandma and then cheered when Elijah, Jeremy, and Rory joined them.

Mrs. Eberlin handed Mom her list of kids. Then Mom read out the names. "I've got Kate, Birdie, Tala, and Julia."

Julia looked hesitant as she strolled over to us. Smiling, I tried to make her feel welcome, but I could tell she wasn't happy about it. She kept on peering over at Mia and Skyler.

"Looks like we've broken up a friend group," Mom whispered. "Sometimes it just can't be helped."

I nodded. It made sense, since not all friends were in groups of four or five. Avery went with her dad, along with Phoenix and two kids from the other class.

"Would it be okay if I stand with Mia and Skyler until we board the bus?" Julia asked my mom.

"Of course," said Mom. "We'll reconvene when we get to the aquarium. After that, we'll be stuck together like superglue."

"Okay, thank you so much!" said Julia, as if my mom had just given her a present. She darted over to be with

Mia and Skyler , and then Mom ran into the school office to do a few last-minute tasks. Meanwhile I zipped open my backpack and pointed at the containers of chocolate-covered pretzels. "We have these!"

After waiting for Tala to join us, we started handing out two pretzel rods to all of the kids. Of course, Memito and Jeremy were first, and they held their pretzels out like swords as they wanted to duel it out.

Next was Julia. "Have a couple of pretzels," offered Birdie.

Julia waved her hand. "Sorry. I shouldn't. It's against the rules to eat on the bus."

"Are you sure?" I asked. Actually, that was a dumb question. Julia knew her rules.

"You could eat them now," Tala told her. "Or just save them for later.

"Thanks," said Julia. "That's really nice." She lowered her voice. "I just don't want to get us in trouble."

That's when Mrs. Eberlin stepped up to us. She gazed at the pretzels. She looked over at me, Birdie, and Tala. "They smell delicious," said Mrs. Eberlin. "Thank you, girls, for making them. However," she switched into her teacher voice and announced, "there's no eating on the bus. So either eat your pretzels now, before you get on the bus, or put them away until it's lunchtime at the aquarium."

"I forgot about the no-eating rule," I said to Birdie as we climbed onto the bus to look for an empty seat.

"Me too," said Birdie, as she shrugged her shoulders.

Mom was the last person onto the bus. "I'm really ready for this trip now," she said to me as she stood in the aisle for a moment. "Everything's settled with the office. No more snow in the forecast." She glanced at her watch. "Let's go!" she yelled, throwing her fist in the air before sitting down toward the back of the bus with Elijah's mom.

"Yes!" we cried. With a tug on her lever, the bus driver closed the door.

I glanced back over at Mom to see if she would start telling everyone a bunch of bus rules. But honestly, she was just chatting with Elijah's mom. She was kind of acting like a regular mom.

She looked like one too in her jeans and bright blue sweater. I wondered how many fifth graders had ever seen her in anything other than her typical principal outfits.

107

Nobody was even whispering that the principal was on board. Instead Mrs. Eberlin was the one to remind of us of the general plan, which was to get to the aquarium at 10:30, see the 11:00 aquatic show, then split off into groups with our chaperones. We were then to meet back all together to have lunch in a special room set up for us.

Mrs. Swensen, our bus driver, pointed out exit locations and said there was no switching around seats. She also told us that we have to drive through Indiana to get to Chicago, which is in a whole other state called Illinois. "You get to see three states today!" she exclaimed. Then everyone clapped as we pulled out of the parking lot. Things were definitely looking up. The roads were clear, and Mom said there was no more snow expected in the forecast.

I turned to Birdie. "Wouldn't that be amazing if we got front-row seats at the aquatic show? And the penguins waddled right in front of us and you took some pictures so you could sketch them later?" Birdie had called me last night to let me know her mom was letting her bring her phone to take photos and for emergencies.

"No flash photography," said Julia from the seat behind us.

"I wouldn't," said Birdie.

"Good, because it's not allowed." Oh brother. She really did have all the rules memorized.

Then suddenly, I heard someone singing "Ninety-Nine Bottles of Milk on the Wall" in the back of the bus. Someone whose voice I knew really well.

My jaw dropped.

It was my mom.

She cupped her ear. "C'mon, everyone. I can't hear you!"

And so with each verse, we all started singing louder and with more energy.

When we got to "one bottle of milk on the wall," we were all singing so loudly they could probably hear us all the way in Chicago.

Kids were laughing, and I could even hear Jeremy say, "The principal is sort of fun."

Yup. That was something I already knew.

Suddenly, Birdie said, "Oh no!"

"What's the matter? Are you car sick? I mean, bus sick?"

"No. The ginger is working. I'm fine. It's just that I spotted a traffic jam ahead."

Sure enough, all at once, the bus suddenly slowed down.

"Are we there?" shouted a kid from the back.

I glanced at my watch. Not possible. It's over two hours to the aquarium, and we'd already been traveling for an hour and a half. We had just crossed the border into Indiana, which I would guess is still an hour from the aquarium, without traffic.

"Maybe traffic will clear up," said Elijah.

But it didn't.

After ten minutes the bus had barely budged.

"Maybe it's an accident," said someone else.

"Welcome to Chicago," said a dad in the front. "It's called the morning commute."

"Not quite," said the bus driver. "It's called I-94. There's always traffic on this highway."

"If we get there late, we won't be able to see the penguin show," said Julia. "Our reservations are for eleven a.m. If we miss it, then we'll just have to skip it."

"Is that true?" I asked Mrs. Eberlin.

"I'm afraid so," she said. "They have school visits scheduled at certain times, so it's not always so flexible, especially on busy days when everyone wants to visit the aquarium." Which is pretty much every day since it's such an awesome place.

That couldn't happen. I wanted to see the show so badly that I could burst like sodium in water.

I looked out the window, and we still hadn't moved.

Wait a minute.

I suddenly remembered something. Sea lions diverge from their migration route if it helps them. For example, I read that more and more sea lions now hunt for salmon in the Columbia River in Oregon because the fish are so plentiful there.

If sea lions could figure out a strategic detour, then we could too.

"Couldn't we find a detour?" I said to my friends, pointing to the exit a quarter mile away.

"You mean like use GPS?" asked Tala. "It uses satellites to figure out how to avoid traffic. Just another reason why satellites are awesome."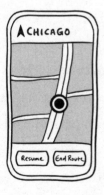

"Yes!" I cried. "Do you think there is another road we can take?"

Birdie whipped out her phone. "If this isn't an emergency, I don't know what is," she said.

She opened up the maps app and started looking for an alternative route.

By now, lots of fifth graders were staring at her and shouting at her to go faster. She started to get flustered and tossed the phone into my hands like a hot potato.

I grabbed her phone and started searching for a better route. "What about US-20?" I asked the bus driver.

"Sure," she said. "But the school only authorized me to go one way, and I can't veer off the path."

"Pleeeeease!" we all begged.

"I'll give you a chocolate-covered pretzel," offered Tala.

"That's very sweet of you, but I have to follow the agreed-upon route," said Mrs. Swensen.

"What if you think of it like an experiment?" I bargained. "We could act like a catalyst! Catalysts are just molecules that speed up a reaction by taking an alternate pathway, like a shortcut."

"Nice try," said the bus driver. "But I have to stay on the path authorized by the school."

The bus grew quiet for a moment before we heard a loud voice from the back.

"I think maybe I can solve that problem."

I turned and looked at my mom walking up from the back of the bus.

"Oh yeah," shouted Elijah. "Luckily, the principal is on the bus!"

She asked the bus driver for the alternative route before checking the directions on her phone. "The route looks safe to me, and it will *definitely* get us to the Shedd Aquarium on schedule." Mom smiled at the driver and then at me.

She didn't need to say anything more. We would barely make it in time to see the penguins at the aquatic show.

CHAPTER EIGHTEEN

AN UNEXPECTED MOVE

Energy Transfer (noun). This is a process where energy moves from one spot to another. So it would be like if you raced around the corner and accidentally slammed into another person. Your energy would transfer to them and send them flying backward. Oops!

WE ALL CHEERED as the aquarium came into view. The enormous building sat right on Lake Michigan, and the Chicago skyline was nearby.

I glanced at my watch. It was 10:58 a.m. "Did we make it in time for the show?" I asked.

"I don't know," Birdie admitted.

"I hope so," Julia said.

We pulled into a bus turnaround area between some orange cones. The bus screeched to a slow stop. The doors opened, and an aquarium staff member, a tall woman holding a clipboard, climbed onto the bus and greeted us.

"Welcome to the Shedd," she said "I'm Shanice. What school are you with?"

"We're from Franklin," Mrs. Eberlin practically yelled as she frantically told Shanice about our 11:00 a.m. reservation.

"Unfortunately, we're not going to be able to get you guys to the eleven a.m. show in time," Shanice stated. "The amphitheater is at least a five-minute walk from here."

There were some groans, including from me. Birdie

looked like she was going to cry.

"Hmmm," Shanice said. "Let me see what I can do." She stepped off the bus and grabbed her walkie-talkie off her hip. We watched her in silence, trying to pick up bits and pieces of her conversation through the closed bus windows.

I had never heard this many fifth

graders be this quiet for this long in my life. Even Jeremy was remaining silent.

All of a sudden, Shanice shrugged, turned around, and walked back onto the bus. We studied her facial expressions for any hint or clue.

And then Shanice smiled.

"Good news!" she squealed. "Luckily, we can squeeze you into the eleven thirty aquatic show. We had some cancellations. Will that work for you guys?"

"Yes," said Mrs. Eberlin, who had made her way to the front of the bus. But Shanice could barely hear our teacher's answer over the cheers.

"Will there be penguins?" I asked.

"Well, each show is different," said Shanice. "We like to give the animals a break. The show you will be seeing might feature different animals."

"So no penguins?" asked Julia in a quiet voice.

"There might be," said Shanice. "But no promises."

My heart sank. I glanced down at my watch. It was now 11:06 a.m.

"Well, at least we can see penguins at their exhibit," said Birdie. "It's not like they'll disappear."

"True," I said. And that made me think about energy

transfers in chemistry. When something moves from one place to another. Those penguins in the 11:00 a.m. show would just be moving back to their exhibit, and other animals would take their place in the show.

And then I remembered what my dad said about his mindfulness talk. You were supposed to notice the feelings in your chest. And just observe them. I noticed that everything felt tight, so I took a long, deep breath.

"It's all going to be so much fun," said Mom, who had walked to the middle of the bus.

"Yes," I said cheerfully, as I grabbed Birdie's hand.

All around me kids were chatting about what they wanted to visit first. Stingrays, sharks, the touch tank. The beluga whales.

Outside, staffers wearing navy parkas and white caps pushed blue and yellow bins, and gathered all of our lunches. As we hurried out of the bus, they handed us maps.

I took another breath as we strolled past a fountain with a statue of a man holding a giant fish. I was finally at the aquarium with my best friends and my mom. It was going to be awesome.

CHAPTER NINETEEN

ABSOLUTE ZERO

Absolute Zero (noun). This is the coldest possible temperature. Since temperature indicates how fast molecules are moving, molecules at absolute zero would be like the laziest molecules in the world.

"I REALLY HOPE there are penguins in the show," said Julia as we stepped down into the amphitheater.

"Me too," I said. "They might be here somewhere. Since it's a tiny bit chilly in here."

"It's absolutely freezing," said Julia, shivering. "Like absolute zero."

"Um, that's not quite possible," Tala said. "Absolute zero is the coldest possible temperature. Where there is no heat at all. And astronomers haven't even discovered that in outer space. I think it's hot in here," she added.

"Are you sure you're really from California?" I said, and we all laughed.

"Well, whatever sea creatures we see, it will be wonderful," Mom said. And it wasn't hard to agree once I looked around. Even though we were inside, it felt like we weren't. Giant boulders surrounded the amphitheater. A wall painted sky blue with fluffy white clouds rose behind a giant tank with sparkling water. On the far left of the tank there was even what looked like a rocky island with pine trees.

"Oh, you know this is going to be good," said Birdie, as we sat down on what looked like stone steps, which were our seats. We were right in front of the huge tank of water. The only thing separating us was a walkway and a clear acrylic divider. "We're super close, which means we're going to get wet!" We all cheered, except for Julia.

"You sure will," said a Shedd staffer in a blue polo and khakis.

"Not me," said Julia. Out of her backpack, she pulled a clear plastic poncho.

"Wow. You came prepared," I said.

"I'm impressed," said Tala.

"I'm kind of looking forward to getting wet," Birdie

admitted as a Shedd emcee's voice boomed out of the speakers.

"Welcome to Shedd's aquatic presentation," the emcee said as everyone quieted down. "You're going to get a closer look at the animals in Shedd's care. During the presentation, I hope you'll join in and have fun as you learn more about these extraordinary animals and how they thrive in nature. We do ask for no flash photography for the safety of the animals. Before we get started, I'd like to get to know a little bit more about you. So on the count of three, everyone shout out where you're visiting from."

We all shouted that we were from Michigan. Other school groups were from Chicago and other parts of Illinois. And I heard some kids yell Indiana and Iowa too.

Then dolphins started swimming around. "Guess the first animal in the show is dolphins," I said, whispering to Birdie as the graceful dolphins started arcing out of the water. We soon learned how dolphins are uniquely adapted for life in the water. The far wall behind the tank became like a screen showing how a dolphin's flippers help them to steer.

As dolphins powered up for some acrobatic jumps,

they made huge splashes, and we definitely got a little wet. There were also trainers in wet suits standing on a rock island in the middle of the pool. It was awesome.

When they asked for a volunteer—"someone who can jump up really high"—I raised my hand as far as I could. "Me! Me!"

The emcee picked a kid with red hair and glasses from another school. After saying his name was Sam, the host told him to jump the highest he had ever jumped in his life.

We counted down: "Three. Two. One." Then he jumped.

"Awesome," said the emcee. "That was probably about a foot. Guess what? These Pacific white-sided dolphins can jump twenty feet."

I believed it. After learning more about the dolphins, we had one last look at the mammals while music played and the screen was lit up by bubbles. Everyone was clapping along.

Next a trainer brought out a raptor. Everyone quieted down as she explained it was a red-tailed hawk. I thought it was cool how the aquarium had birds. I wasn't expecting that at all.

When it flapped its wings, I was amazed at the wingspan. "I'd like one of those in the office during the summer," Mom joked. "If it flapped its wings, I wouldn't need a fan."

After we learned some cool facts about the hawk, like how its eyesight is eight times better than humans', the host said we should get ready for our last animal.

"What is it?" someone called out from the back.

"You'll see," said the emcee. "Okay, everyone. We're going to have some animals joining us on the walkway, and so I want everyone to remain seated and stay calm."

"Oh, I wonder what it will be?" said Tala.

"Maybe whales?" suggested Memito from behind me.

I laughed. "Last time I looked whales can't walk on land."

"Maybe they put them on giant skateboards," said Elijah, and we all cracked up. But I was so excited I was biting my fingernails.

"I really, really hope it's penguins," I said.

"Me too," said Julia.

"Okay, everyone," said the emcee. "Let's give it up for our special guests." All of us looked at the walkway, and I couldn't believe my eyes. Because this animal was ridiculously cute.

CHAPTER TWENTY

FUN AND GAMES

Polymer Chemistry (noun). The part of chemistry that studies really big molecules called polymers. Most plastics are actually just made of humongous polymers. So if you were a polymer chemist, you could study how to make a plastic ball like the kind sea lions play with at an aquarium.

"LET'S GIVE IT UP FOR FINN!" shouted the emcee, as the cutest sea lion you ever saw walked right past us. And I mean right in front of us. I could have leaned over and petted him.

"Finn is a California sea lion," continued the emcee. "These marine mammals are related to seals and walruses." Wow. I didn't realize that sea lions were related to walruses. That could be one of my super-duper facts.

"That's my animal!" I said, pumping my fist into

the air. "I mean, not like I own him or anything," I murmured. "I'm doing a presentation on sea lions on Monday."

"That's great," said the emcee. "All the sea lions at the aquarium were rescued. We have four altogether. Biff, Tanner, Laguna, and Finn right here. Sometimes Finn likes to be a whirlybird." Finn started to spin in circles. He was really acrobatic and elegant. "He can't use his eyes, because he is blind."

She explained that he had shrapnel in his eyes because he had been shot. That part was really sad.

Lots of kids made an *ooh* sound, including me.

But she explained that Finn had adapted really well and was happy and thriving and loved to play with balls, especially a green plastic one. I thought about how it was probably made from polymers, which are really just ginormous molecules.

"When we're training the other sea lions, we give hand motions, but with Finn it's all verbal and he understands everything. Don't you, buddy?"

And with that, he gave his trainer a high five. It was amazing. Finn certainly didn't act like he didn't know what was going on or where he was going.

"Any questions?" asked the emcee.

"What does he eat?" asked Memito.

"A variety of herring, squid, capelin, and sometimes salmon," said the emcee.

"How does he follow the trainer?" I asked. "And swim around?"

"He has whiskers that help him feel around," she said. "He knows his habitat really well because he has it all mapped out in his head."

"That's so cool." I thought of the GPS that got us here. It was like he had a mapping service in his brain. Okay, I had my second super-duper fact. Then we learned some things about how sea lions are threatened. Not only by hunting, but they also get caught in nets and plastic. And pollution and overfishing are other problems. Which also made me sad.

"Luckily, our animal response team works with conservation partners around the globe to rescue animals like Finn," said the emcee, and everyone clapped at that happy news.

The trainer held what looked like a wand with a red bulb, which was for training. For Finn, she would tap him with the bulb and he would lie down. "He feels like a wet horse," the emcee said, as the trainer touched him. "He likes rubs. Especially on his chest. He also likes Jell-O with no taste or flavor. And playing with ice."

Oh my. I started to write everything down in my notebook. I had so many super-duper facts. Way more than three.

Lifting up a flipper, Finn waved goodbye, and I was waving good-bye too. Even though I knew he couldn't see me, I was sure he could hear me. "Bye, Finn!" I shouted.

That was so wonderful.

"I bet you're going to have a lot of questions," said the emcee. "Which is good. Anytime you see a staffer, do not hesitate to ask us anything. Stay sea curious. And you can learn a lot just by observing."

She went on to explain that we'd start with general explorations of the galleries upstairs. "I'd recommend starting with either the Great Lakes or the Wild Reef, which you will need to take elevators to get to. It's not an aquarium without a shark tank, and there are plenty of them in the Wild Reef."

Then we all turned to each other. "Where should we go first, Mrs. Crawford?" asked Julia.

"I think you all should decide what you want to see."

"Let's try the Wild Reef," said Birdie, "and then maybe the Great Lakes."

"And then the penguins," said Julia and I practically at the same time.

Even though the aquatic show had been different from what we planned, it still had been absolutely amazing. I almost touched a sea lion!

"Okay, everyone," I said. "It's time to check out those exhibits." I couldn't wait to find out what else we would see.

CHAPTER TWENTY-ONE

QUITE A SIGHT!

Magnetic Field (noun). An area where an object has the ability to have an influence on something else, which it can repel or attract. Think of it like how if you held up a lollipop, you'd attract your friend. And if you held up a dead fish, they'd probably turn and run the other way.

THE WILD REEF WAS AMAZING. Especially the zebra sharks. I couldn't take my eyes off them. They were all stripes and spots and swam around so elegantly. They live in tropical waters around reefs. Tala was especially taken with what looked like an eel tucked into some tunnels. She said he was like a magnet, and she couldn't take her eyes off him.

We passed by Memito's grandmother followed by Elijah, Memito, Rory, and Jeremy. Amazingly, Jeremy said he'd gotten the best super-duper fact about a parrotfish.

"It's the coolest 'cause it covers itself in slime to go to sleep. Like snot pajamas."

"That's gross," said Memito.

"No way! They do it for protection from parasites," said Jeremy. "It's awesome!"

What was also awesome was the Great Lakes exhibit and the jellies, which looked like they were dancing and doing ballet. Those were Birdie's words, of course.

But most of all, I couldn't wait to see my rockhopper penguins. I followed the signs, and sure enough, there they were.

"Look! Look!" Behind the thick glass, there were so many penguins busy swimming in the water or waddling

around. The aquarium had two kinds: Magellanic and rockhoppers. The Magellanics were black and white and had such a cute waddle. And they were about a half a foot taller than the rockhoppers. The rockhoppers had orange beaks and little yellow tufts above their eyes and hopped and bounced around. The water was so clear and blue, and the penguins had all kinds of nooks and crannies to hang out in.

"I wonder if they play hide-and-seek," mused Tala.

"Girls, look," said Mom. "That penguin is following the other one. Kate, it reminds me of you and Liam when you were younger."

Birdie whipped out her phone to take photos for me. "Kate, I'll send you the pics when we get home. You've got to remember this cuteness."

"Isn't this the best?" I shouted to Julia, sure that she would be happy. But instead she was intently reading everything. And looking glum. As Mom moved farther down the exhibit to check out some diving penguins with Tala, I noticed that Julia was definitely frowning.

"What's the matter?" I asked her.

"I know everything," she said.

"What do you mean?"

"We were supposed to find three super-duper facts. Something new that we learned at the aquarium. But with my research, I've already learned everything here." She pointed to the information on the signs posted around the exhibit.

"Are you sure?"

She started listing facts. How penguins have fused bones. How they sneeze to get rid of salt in the water that they drink. How Magellanic penguins can swim fifteen miles per hour. How the rockhoppers make nests out of rocks. Wow. She really had done a lot of research after all. I was impressed that she knew way more than she used to back when she wanted penguins to be magenta.

She started to pace. "What am I going to do?" she asked. "How am going to get my presentation done?"

"Well, I know lots of facts about penguins," I said. "I could tell you some facts and—"

Julia shook her head. "No," she said. "Those aren't the rules. We're supposed to learn something new at the Shedd."

I sighed. "But you're learning from me, and we're at the Shedd."

Julia folded her arms. "I don't think that's a good idea."

"You're not being flexible," I said in a voice that maybe was a little too sharp.

"Neither are you," she said. "You've been mad at me ever since I picked penguins as my sea creature to study."

"That's not—"

"It is," she said.

I hung my head. "You're right. It's true. It's just that I love them so much. I even have posters of rockhoppers up in my bedroom."

"Well, I didn't know anything about penguins. And I wanted to learn."

"That's actually really cool," I admitted. "I've enjoyed learning about sea lions, to tell you the truth. I'm sorry if I've been grumpy. And I'm sorry that you're having trouble finding your super-duper facts."

Then at that moment Shanice walked by with her crackling walkie-talkie, and I had an idea. "The emcee said we're supposed to be sea curious and to ask a staff person our questions. Let's ask Shanice."

We both raced up to Shanice and asked her if she knew any more information about penguins. A huge smile stretched across her face. "I do," she said. "But I know someone who knows even more than me. They are going to be feeding the penguins in about twenty minutes. But the trainers like to get to the exhibit early. Since you all missed that penguin show this morning, I can introduce you to the trainers and you can ask some questions."

"Really?" I asked.

"Yes," said Shanice. "See, here they come." And sure enough, she pointed to a couple of trainers starting to enter the exhibit.

I stared at the trainers with their buckets. Getting to talk to them would be so awesome.

"Girls," said Mom. She looked at her phone. "We better leave now if you want to get anything at the gift store. We have less than twenty minutes before we have to board the bus to go home."

"Already? Wow. I feel like we just got here," said Tala.

"Me too," said Birdie, looking at her sketchpad. "But I definitely want to get some souvenirs."

"Same," said Tala.

"I actually wanted to get a penguin T-shirt," admitted Julia.

"There won't be time to talk with the trainers and go to the gift store," said Mom. "As a group we're going to have to choose one or the other."

"Then I pick staying with the trainers," stated Julia.

Mom glanced at Shanice, and then she studied her phone. "I'll tell you what," said Mom. "I'll stay here with Julia, and whoever wants to go to the gift shop can go. It's right around the corner, and Elijah's mom just texted me that her group is there."

"I'd like to go to the gift shop," said Tala.

"Me too," added Birdie.

Mom flicked a glance at me. "Kate, are you going to stay?"

I studied the exhibit and swallowed. I thought about my promise to Liam to pick out the perfect stuffed animal, hopefully an awesome cephalopod. And how I also wanted a T-shirt. "No, I'm going to the gift store," I said. "And if you give me your money, Julia, I can buy you the penguin shirt."

"Wow. Thanks so much," said Julia, and she handed me twenty dollars and told me she wore a kids' large.

Then Tala, Birdie, and I made our way to the gift

shop as I took one last look at an adorable rockhopper who was bouncing along the rocks. "See you all back at the bus!" said Shanice.

Then I thought about Finn, who had been through so much.

And he was so playful and had figured out how to adapt.

I realized something. I already knew a lot about penguins.

But I didn't know so much about sea lions.

And it was sometimes important to adapt. Even if some of the changes weren't what you wanted.

I had wanted to do my report on penguins.

But now I was really glad that I was doing my presentation on sea lions.

But I still really wanted to get my penguin T-shirt, and Liam his stuffed octopus toy. My heart felt all fluttery and happy thinking about that. Soon enough I'd have a T-shirt like all my friends to celebrate a wonderful day.

CHAPTER TWENTY-TWO

GO WiTH THE FLOW

Molecular Flexibility (noun). This is the ability for molecules to be flexible. For example, in a rubber ball the molecules are in long chains and are weakly linked together. That's why rubber is elastic and bounces—because the molecules can wiggle around to adapt to the motion of slamming into the ground.

AT THE GIFT STORE, there were so many things to look at. Books, posters, shirts, and lots of stuffed animals. Elijah's mom was in the book section, buying a stack of books to donate to the library collection at our school.

Very quickly, I was able to find this adorable stuffed octopus for Liam. It had these cute arms that he would love to snuggle with at night.

Tala found an awesome poster featuring sea stars. "It will look so perfect in my room," she said. "Right next to my posters of the constellations of regular stars."

And Birdie was over by a section where they had some art supplies with aquatic themes. "Aren't these colored pencils nice?" she said. The lid had a scene of a coral reef.

"Definitely."

I glanced at my watch. We only had seven minutes before we needed to leave. I raced over to the T-shirt section.

For the next few minutes, I searched for penguin shirts in my size, which was the same as Julia's. Penguins must be popular, because they didn't have a huge selection.

"Oh no," I said, flipping through the stack of shirts. "There's a big problem."

"What is it?" said Birdie.

"There's only one kids' large left." I bit my bottom lip. "And Julia wanted me to get her one too." I could tell her the truth that there was only one left and because she had stayed with the penguins, I had taken the shirt.

No. I couldn't do that.

It didn't feel right. I would never do that to Birdie or Tala. And I couldn't do that to Julia either.

Next to the penguins were the sea lion T-shirts. The image on one looked just like Finn, the sea lion who knew how to adapt and how to have fun. I thought about how much I'd loved meeting him that morning and how much I'd learned about sea lions. I took a deep breath. "I'm going to get this one instead," I said, pulling out one in my size.

"Are you sure?" asked Birdie.

I paused for a second. But I was sure. I just had to be flexible, like molecules in matter. They have to bend and twist to adapt to their environment, and I was just going to have to do that too.

"Completely," I said. "When we come back this summer, I can get a penguin shirt."

"Or maybe I can make one for you," said Birdie. "Based on my photos."

"Wow," I said. "That would be so cool." We went up to the cashier. First, I got Julia her shirt. The cashier gave me back the change, which I put in my pocket for Julia. Then I gave the cashier my shirt and

Liam's octopus. "That will be forty-two dollars," said the cashier.

Forty-two dollars? I can't believe I forgot to look at the price tags. I pulled out my ten ones and six five-dollar bills. I was two dollars short. I looked at the money in my hand, and then I looked at the cashier. If only my mom had come, I could have asked her for the two dollars.

"I . . . um . . . I don't have enough." I thought about Liam and how excited he would be to get the octopus. There was no way I could go home without it. "I guess I have to put away the shirt," I said as I started to turn away from the cashier.

"No, you don't," said Birdie, walking up next to me, and she plunked down two dollars. "I got you."

"You really don't have to do that," I told her.

"I know," she said. "But I'm doing it anyway."

"Thanks," I said.

"That's what best friends are for," she added, and then she paid for her coral reef–themed colored pencils too. I thought about which chores I could do that weekend so I could pay her back. Maybe not with two dollars, but with a gift that she would really love. Maybe some special art paper for her colored pencils. Or some homemade brownies. I wanted her to know that I appreciated how great a friend she was. Always.

Birdie took her bag from the cashier, and then we joined hands and skipped back to the bus.

"I'm super glad I saved my pretzels," I said. "We can share them quickly before boarding."

"Yum," said Birdie, biting into the salty-sweet snack. "It's so good."

"Just like our day at the aquarium," I said.

We met some animals, we learned some science, but most of all, we got to spend some time with our friends.

CHOCOLATE-COVERED PRETZELS

Materials:

☆ Baking sheet
☆ Parchment paper (or nonstick cooking spray or silicone baking mat)
☆ 4 ounces white baking chocolate
☆ 4 small microwave-safe bowls
☆ 4 tablespoons vegetable shortening
☆ Microwave
☆ 1 bag of pretzel rods
☆ 4 ounces unsweetened baking chocolate (100% cacao)
☆ 4 ounces semi-sweet baking chocolate (56% cacao)
☆ 4 ounces milk chocolate baking chocolate (32% cacao)
☆ Refrigerator

Protocol:

1. Prepare a baking sheet (spray with nonstick cooking spray or line with parchment paper or silicone baking mat).

2. Break up the white chocolate into small, bite-size pieces.

3. Place it into Bowl 1.

4. Add 1 tablespoon of vegetable shortening to Bowl 1.

5. Microwave Bowl 1 for 30 seconds.

6. Remove from the microwave. Analyze the appearance of the chocolate and then stir.

7. Continue to microwave the chocolate in 10-second increments (stirring after each session) until all of the chocolate has melted. Record your observations.

8. Dip the pretzel rod into the melted chocolate and rotate to coat evenly. PRO TIP: Use a basting brush to brush the chocolate onto the pretzel for more even coverage.

9. Place the pretzel on the baking sheet.

10. Repeat steps 8–9 for four more pretzel rods. MINI-EXPERIMENT: Consider brushing the salt off one of the pretzels before dipping it in chocolate. You can compare the way the chocolate sticks to the unsalted pretzel versus the ones with salt.

11. Repeat steps 2–10 for each of the other chocolates. Do your best to break up each of the chocolates into similar-size pieces. Make sure to record the total time it takes for each chocolate to melt, and describe the final appearance of each chocolate on the pretzels.

12. Place the baking sheet in the refrigerator for 20–30 minutes (until all of the chocolate has solidified).

13. Compare the final products and then share your Chocolate-Covered Pretzels with your friends and family!

HOW IT WORKS:

Vegetable shortening is made of triglyceride molecules that exist in the solid phase. The term *shortening* is a generic term that can be used for any type of fat that exists as a solid at room temperature. It first earned its name back in the nineteenth century, when it was used to shorten dough. The shortening disrupted the bonds within the dough, which made the resulting baked goods taste light and flaky.

Vegetable shortening is a specific type of shortening that is made from vegetable oil. Traditionally, vegetable oil is made of triglyceride molecules that have one double bond. However, manufacturers can hydrogenate vegetable oil—basically, they add hydrogen to it—which converts that double bond into a single bond. When this happens, the vegetable *oil* turns into vegetable *shortening* (fat), which is a much better ingredient for pies.

When the vegetable shortening starts to melt in the microwave, the surrounding chocolate melts too. Lighter chocolates (like white chocolate and milk chocolate) melt at lower temperatures, around 40–45°C (104–113°F), whereas darker chocolates melt at higher temperatures, around 45–50°C (113–122°F). These melting points are a direct result of how much cocoa is in the original chocolate. The more cocoa a chocolate has, the higher its melting point will be.

DR. Kate Biberdorf, also known as Kate the Chemist by her fans, is a science professor at UT–Austin by day and a science superhero by night (well, she does that by day, too). Kate travels the country building a STEM army of kids who love science as much as she does. You can often find her breathing fire or making slime—always in her lab coat and goggles.

You can visit Kate on Instagram and Facebook @KatetheChemist, on Twitter @K8theChemist, and online at KatetheChemist.com.

DON'T MISS ANY OF KATE'S ADVENTURES!

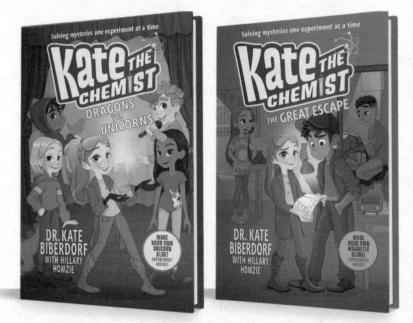

Become a scientist like